ALL THE WRONG QUESTIONS
1

"Who Could That Be at This Hour?"

LEMONY SNICKET

ART BY SETH

Little, Brown and Company
New York Boston

Little, Brown and Company

Hachette Book Group / 237 Park Avenue, New York, NY 10017
Visit our website at www.lb-kids.com

Little, Brown and Company is a division of Hachette Book Group, Inc. The Little, Brown name and logo are trademarks of Hachette Book Group, Inc.

The publisher is not responsible for websites (or their content) that are not owned by the publisher.

First Edition: October 2012

ISBN 978-0-316-12308-2

10 9 8 7 6 5 4 3 2 1

RRD-H / Printed in the United States of America

ALL THE WRONG
QUESTIONS

?

1

"Who Could That Be at This Hour?"

CHAPTER ONE

There was a town, and there was a girl, and there was a theft. I was living in the town, and I was hired to investigate the theft, and I thought the girl had nothing to do with it. I was almost thirteen and I was wrong. I was wrong about all of it. I should have asked the question "Why would someone say something was stolen when it was never theirs to begin with?" Instead, I asked the wrong question—four wrong questions, more or less. This is the account of the first.

The Hemlock Tearoom and Stationery Shop is the sort of place where the floors always feel dirty, even when they are clean. They were not clean on the day in question. The food at the Hemlock is too awful to eat, particularly the eggs, which are probably the worst eggs in the entire city, including those on exhibit at the Museum of Bad Breakfast, where visitors can learn just how badly eggs can be prepared. The Hemlock sells paper and pens that are damaged and useless, but the tea is drinkable, and the place is located across the street from the train station, so it is an acceptable place to sit with one's parents before boarding a train for a new life. I was wearing the suit I'd been given as a graduation present. It had hung in my closet for weeks, like an empty person. I felt glum and thirsty. When the tea arrived, for a moment the steam was all I could see. I'd said good-bye to someone very quickly and was wishing I'd taken longer. I told myself that it didn't matter and that certainly it was no time to frown around town. You have work to do, Snicket, I told myself. There is no time for moping.

You'll see her soon enough in any case, I thought, incorrectly.

Then the steam cleared, and I looked at the people who were with me. It is curious to look at one's family and try to imagine how they look to strangers. I saw a large-shouldered man in a brown, linty suit that looked like it made him uncomfortable, and a woman drumming her fingernails on the table, over and over, the sound like a tiny horse's galloping. She happened to have a flower in her hair. They were both smiling, particularly the man.

"You have plenty of time before your train, son," he said. "Would you like to order something to eat? Eggs?"

"No, thank you," I said.

"We're both so proud of our little boy," said

the woman, who perhaps would have looked nervous to someone who was looking closely at her. Or perhaps not. She stopped drumming her fingers on the table and ran them through my hair. Soon I would need a haircut. "You must be all a-tingle with excitement."

"I guess so," I said, but I did not feel a-tingle. I did not feel a-anything.

"Put your napkin in your lap," she told me.

"I did."

"Well, then, drink your tea," she said, and another woman came into the Hemlock. She did not look at me or my family or anywhere at all. She brushed by my table, very tall, with a very great deal of very wild hair. Her shoes made noise on the floor. She stopped at a rack of envelopes and grabbed the first one she saw, tossing a coin to the woman behind the counter, who caught it almost without looking, and then she was back out the door. With all the tea on all the tables, it looked like one of her pockets was steaming. I was the only one who had noticed her. She did not look back.

There are two good reasons to put your napkin in your lap. One is that food might spill in your lap, and it is better to stain the napkin than your clothing. The other is that it can serve as a perfect hiding place. Practically nobody is nosy enough to take the napkin off a lap to see what is hidden there. I sighed deeply and stared down at my lap, as if I were lost in thought, and then quickly and quietly I unfolded and read the note the woman had dropped there.

CLIMB OUT THE WINDOW IN THE
BATHROOM AND MEET ME IN THE ALLEY
BEHIND THIS SHOP. I WILL BE WAITING
IN THE GREEN ROADSTER. YOU HAVE
FIVE MINUTES. —S

"Roadster," I knew, was a fancy word for "car," and I couldn't help but wonder what kind of person would take the time to write "roadster" when the word "car" would do. I also couldn't help but wonder what sort of person would sign a secret note, even if they only signed the letter *S*. A secret note is secret. There is no reason to sign it.

"Are you OK, son?"

"I need to excuse myself," I said, and stood up. I put the napkin down on the table but kept the note crumpled up in my hand.

"Drink your tea."

"*Mother*," I said.

"Let him go, dear," said the man in the brown suit. "He's almost thirteen. It's a difficult age."

I stood up and walked to the back of the Hemlock. Probably one minute had passed already. The woman behind the counter watched me look this way and that. In restaurants they always make you ask where the bathroom is, even when there's nothing else you could be looking for. I told myself not to be embarrassed.

"If I were a bathroom," I said to the woman, "where would I be?"

She pointed to a small hallway. I noticed the coin was still in her hand. I stepped quickly down the hallway without looking back. I would not see the Hemlock Tearoom and Stationery Shop again for years and years.

I walked into the bathroom and saw that I was not alone. I could think of only two things to do in a bathroom while waiting to be alone. I did one of them, which was to stand at the sink and splash some cold water on my face. I took the opportunity to wrap the note in a paper towel and then run the thing under the water so it was a wet mess. I threw it away. Probably nobody would look for it.

A man came out of the stall and caught my eye in the mirror. "Are you all right?" he asked me. I must have looked nervous.

"I had the eggs," I said, and he washed his hands sympathetically and left. I turned off the water and looked at the only window. It was small and square and had a very simple latch. A child could open it, which was good, because I was a child. The problem was that it was ten feet above me, in a high corner of the bathroom. Even standing on tiptoes, I couldn't reach the point where I'd have to stand if I wanted to reach the point to open the latch. Any age was a difficult age for someone needing to get through that window.

I walked into the bathroom stall. Behind the toilet was a large parcel wrapped in brown paper and string, but wrapped loosely, as if nobody cared whether you opened it or not. Leaned up against the wall like that, it didn't look interesting. It looked like something the Hemlock needed, or a piece of equipment a plumber had left behind. It looked like none of your business. I dragged it into the middle of the stall and shut the door behind me as I tore open the paper. I didn't lock it. A man with large shoulders could force open a door like that even if it were locked.

It was a folding ladder. I knew it was there. I'd put it there myself.

It was probably one minute to find the note, one to walk to the bathroom, one to wait for the man to leave, and two to set up the ladder, unlatch the window, and half-jump, half-slide out the window into a small puddle in the alley. That's five minutes. I brushed muddy water off my pants. The roadster was small and green and looked like it had once been a race car, but now it had cracks and creaks all along its curved body. The roadster had been neglected. No one had taken care of it, and now it was too late. The woman was frowning behind the steering wheel

9

when I got in. Her hair was now wrestled into place by a small leather helmet. The windows were rolled down, and the rainy air matched the mood in the car.

"I'm S. Theodora Markson," she said.

"I'm Lemony Snicket," I said, and handed her an envelope I had in my pocket. Inside was something we called a letter of introduction, just a few paragraphs describing me as somebody who was an excellent reader, a good cook, a mediocre musician, and an awful quarreler. I had been instructed not to read my letter of introduction, and it had taken me some time to slip the envelope open and then reseal it.

"I know who you are," she said, and tossed the envelope into the backseat. She was staring through the windshield like we were already on the road. "There's been a change of plans. We're in a great hurry. The situation is more complicated than you understand or than I am in a position to explain to you under the present circumstances."

"Under the present circumstances," I repeated. "You mean, right now?"

"Of course that's what I mean."

"If we're in a great hurry, why didn't you just say 'right now'?"

She reached across my lap and pushed open the door. "Get out," she said.

"What?"

"I will not be spoken to this way. Your predecessor, the young man who worked under me before you, he never spoke to me this way. *Never.* Get out."

"I'm sorry," I said.

"Get out."

"I'm sorry," I said.

"Do you want to work under me, Snicket? Do you want me to be your chaperone?"

I stared out at the alley. "Yes," I said.

"Then know this: I am not your friend. I am not your teacher. I am not a parent or a guardian or anyone who will take care of you. I am your chaperone, and you are my apprentice, a word which here means 'person who works under me and does absolutely everything I tell him to do.'"

"I'm contrite," I said, "a word which here means—"

"You already said you were sorry," S. Theodora Markson said. "Don't repeat yourself. It's not only repetitive, it's redundant, and people have heard it before. It's not proper. It's not sensible. I am S. Theodora Markson. You may call me Theodora or Markson. You are my apprentice. You work under me, and you will do everything I tell you to do. I will call you Snicket. There is no easy way to train an apprentice. My two tools are example and nagging. I will show you what it is I do, and then I will tell you to do other things yourself. Do you under-stand?"

"What's the *S* stand for?"

"Stop asking the wrong questions," she replied, and started the engine. "You probably think you know everything, Snicket. You are probably very proud of yourself for graduating, and for managing to sneak out of a bathroom window in five and a half minutes. But you know nothing."

S. Theodora Markson took one of her gloved hands off the steering wheel and reached up to the dashboard of the roadster. I noticed for the first time a teacup, still steaming. The side of the cup read HEMLOCK.

"You probably didn't even notice I took your tea, Snicket," she said, and then reached across me and dumped the tea out the window. It steamed on the ground, and for a few seconds we watched an eerie cloud rise into the air of the alley. The smell was sweet and wrong, like a dangerous flower.

"Laudanum," she said. "It's an opiate. It's a medicament. It's a sleeping draught." She turned and looked at me for the first time. She looked pleasant enough, I would say, though I wouldn't say it to her. She looked like a woman with a great deal to do, which is what I was counting on. "Three sips of that and you would have been incoherent, a word which here means mumbling crazy talk and nearly unconscious. You never would have caught that train, Snicket. Your parents would have hurried you out of that place and taken you someplace else, someplace I assure you that you do not want to be."

The cloud disappeared, but I kept staring at it. I felt all alone in the alley. If I had drunk my tea, I never would have been in that roadster, and if I had not been in that roadster, I never would have ended up falling into the wrong tree, or walking into the wrong basement, or destroying the wrong library, or finding all the other wrong answers to the wrong questions I was asking. She was right, S. Theodora Markson. There was no one to take care of me. I was hungry. I shut the door of the car and looked her in the eye.

"Those weren't my parents," I said, and off we went.

CHAPTER TWO

If you ask the right librarian and you get the right map, you can find the small dot of a town called Stain'd-by-the-Sea, about half a day's drive from the city. But the town is actually nowhere near the sea but instead at the end of a long, bumpy road that has no name which is on no map you can find. I know this because it was in Stain'd-by-the-Sea that I spent my apprenticeship, and not in the city, where I thought it would be. I did not know this until S. Theodora

Markson drove the roadster past the train station without even slowing down.

"Aren't we taking the train?" I asked.

"That's another wrong question," she said. "I told you there's been a change of plans. The map is not the territory. That's an expression which means the world does not match the picture in our heads."

"I thought we were working across town."

"That's exactly what I mean, Snicket. You *thought* we were working across town, but we are not working in the city at all."

My stomach fell to the floor of the car, which rattled as we took a sharp turn around a construction site. A team of workers were digging up the street to start work on the Fountain of Victorious Finance. Tomorrow, if it were possible for an apprentice to sneak away for lunch, I was supposed to meet someone right there, in hopes of measuring how deep the hole was that they were digging. I'd managed to acquire a new measuring tape for just that purpose, one that stretched out a very long distance and then scurried back into its holder with a satisfying *click*. The holder was shaped like a bat, and the tape measure was red, as if the bat had a very long tongue. I realized I would never see it again.

"My suitcase," I said, "is at the train station."

"I purchased some clothes for you," Theodora said, and tilted her helmeted head toward the backseat, where I saw a small, bruised suitcase. "I was given your measurements, so hopefully they fit. If they don't, you will have to either lose or gain weight or height. They're unremarkable clothes. The idea is not to attract attention."

I thought that wearing clothes either too big or too small for me would be likely to attract attention, and I thought of the small stack of books I had tucked next to the bat. One of them was very important. It was a history of the city's underground sewer system. I had planned to take a few notes on chapter 5 of the book, on the train across town. When I disembarked at Bellamy Station, I would crumple the notes into a ball and toss them to my associate without being seen. She would be standing at the magazine rack at Bellamy Books. It was all mapped out, but now the territory was different. She would read magazines for hours before catching her own train to her own apprenticeship, but then what would she do? What would I do? I scowled out the window and asked myself these and other hopeless questions.

"Your reticence is not appreciated," Theodora said, breaking my sour silence. "'Reticence' is a word which here means not talking enough. Say something, Snicket."

"Are we there yet?" I asked hopefully, although everyone knows that is the wrong question to ask the driver of a car. "Where are we going?" I tried instead, but for a moment Theodora did not answer. She was biting her lip, as if she were also disappointed about something, so I tried one more question that I thought she might like better. "What does the S stand for?"

"Someplace else," she replied, and it was true. Before long we had passed out of the neighborhood, and then out of the district, and then out of the city altogether and were driving along a very twisty road that made me grateful I had eaten little. The air had such a curious smell that we had to close the windows of the roadster, and it looked like rain. I stared out the window and watched the day grow later. Few cars were on the road, but all of them were in better shape than Theodora's. Twice I almost fell asleep thinking of places and people in the city that were dearly important to me, and the distance between them and myself growing and growing until the distance grew so vast that even the longest-tongued bat in the world could not lick the life I was leaving behind.

A new sound rattled me out of my thoughts. The road had become rough and crackly under the vehicle's wheels as Theodora took us down a hill so steep and long I could not see the bottom of it through the roadster's dirty windows.

"We're driving on seashells," my chaperone said in explanation. "This last part of the journey is all seashells and stones."

"Who would pave a road like that?"

"Wrong question, Snicket," she replied. "Nobody paved it, and it's not really a road. This entire valley used to be underwater. It was drained some years back. You can see why it would be absolutely impossible to take the train."

A whistle blew right then. I decided not to say anything. Theodora glared at me anyway and then frowned out the window. A distance away was the hurried, slender shape of a long train, balancing high above the bumpy valley where we were driving. The train tracks were on a long, high bridge, which curved out from the shore to reach an island that was now just a mountain of stones rising out of the drained valley. Theodora turned the roadster toward the island, and as we approached I could see a group of buildings—faded brick buildings enclosed by a faded brick wall. A school, perhaps, or the estate of a dull family. The buildings had once been elegant, but many of the windows were shattered and gone, and there were no signs of life. I was surprised to hear, just as the roadster passed directly under the bridge, the low, loud clanging of a bell, from a high brick tower that looked abandoned and sad on a pile of rocks.

Theodora cleared her throat. "There should be two masks behind you."

"Masks?" I said.

"Don't repeat what I say, Snicket. You are an apprentice, not a mynah bird. There are two masks on the backseat. We need them."

23

I reached back and found the items in question but had to stare at them for a moment before I found the courage to pick them up. The two masks, one for an adult and one for a child, were fashioned from a shiny silver metal, with a tangle of rubber tubes and filters on the back. On the front were narrow slits for the eyes and a small ripple underneath for the nose. There was nothing where a mouth might be, so the faces of the masks looked at me silently and spookily, as if they thought this whole journey was a bad idea.

"I absolutely agree," I told them.

Theodora frowned. "That bell means we should don these masks. 'Don' is a word which here means 'put on our heads.' The pressure at this depth will make it difficult to breathe otherwise."

"Pressure?"

"Water pressure, Snicket. It's everywhere

around us. Masked or not, you must use your head."

My head told me it didn't understand how there could be water pressure everywhere around us. There wasn't any water. I wondered where all the water had gone when they'd drained this part of the sea, and I should have wondered. But I told myself it was the wrong question and asked something else instead. "Why did they do this? Why did they drain the sea of its water?"

S. Theodora Markson took one mask from my hands and slipped it onto her helmeted head. "To save the town," she replied in a muffled voice. "Put your mask on, Snicket."

I did as Theodora said. The mask was dark inside and smelled faintly like a cave or a closet that had not been opened in some time. A few tubes huddled in front of my mouth, like worms in front of a fish. I blinked behind the slits at Theodora, who blinked back.

"Is the mask working?" she asked me.

"How can I tell?"

"If you can breathe, then it's working."

I did not say that I had been breathing previously. Something more interesting had attracted my attention. Out the window of the roadster I saw a line of big barrels, round and old, squatting uncovered next to some odd, enormous machines. The machines looked like huge hypodermic needles, as if a doctor were planning on giving several shots to a giant. Here and there were people—men or women, it was impossible to tell in their masks—checking on the needles to make sure they were working properly. They were. With a swinging of hinges and a turning of gears, the needles plunged deep into holes in the shell-covered ground and then rose up again, full of a black liquid. The needles deposited the liquid, with a quiet black splash, into the barrels and then plunged back into the holes, over and over again while I watched through the slits in my mask.

"Oil," I guessed.

"Ink," Theodora corrected. "The town is called Stain'd-by-the-Sea. Of course, it is no longer by the sea, as they've drained it away. But the town still manufactures ink that was once famous for making the darkest, most permanent stains."

"And the ink is in those holes?"

"Those holes are long, narrow caves," Theodora said, "like wells. And in the caves are octopi. That's where the ink comes from."

I thought of a friend of mine who had also just graduated, a girl who knew about all sorts of underwater life. "I thought octopi make ink only when they are frightened."

"I imagine an octopus would find those machines very frightening indeed," Theodora

27

said, and she turned the roadster onto a narrow path in the shells that twisted upward, climbing a steep and craggy mountain. At its peak, I could see a faint, pulsing light through the afternoon gray. It took me a minute to realize that it was a lighthouse, which stood on a cliff that overlooked what had been waves and water and was now just a vast, eerie landscape. As the roadster sputtered up the hill, I looked out the windows on Theodora's side and saw that opposite the inkwells was another strange sight.

"The Clusterous Forest," Theodora said, before I could even ask. "When they drained the sea, everyone thought all of the seaweed would shrivel up and die. But my information says that for some mysterious reason, the seaweed learned to grow on dry land, and now for miles and miles there is an enormous forest of seaweed. Never go in there, Snicket. It is a wild and lawless place, not fit for man or beast."

She did not have to tell me not to go into the Clusterous Forest. It was frightening enough just to look at it. It was less like a forest and more like an endless mass of shrubbery, with the shiny leaves of the seaweed twisting this way and that, as if the plants were still under churning water. Even with the windows shut, I could smell the forest, a brackish scent of fish and soil, and I could hear the rustling of thousands of strands of seaweed that had somehow survived the draining of the sea.

The bell rang again as the roadster finally reached the top of the hill, signaling the all-clear. We removed our masks, and Theodora steered the car onto an actual paved road that wound past the blinking lighthouse and down a hill lined with trees. We passed a small white cottage and then came to a stop at the driveway of a mansion so large it looked like several mansions had crashed together. Parts of it looked like a castle, with several tall towers stretching high into the cloudy air, and parts of it looked like a tent, with heavy gray cloth stretched over an ornate garden crawling with fountains and statues, and parts of it looked more like a museum, with a severe front door and a long, long stretch of window. The view from the window must have been very pretty once, with the waves crashing below the cliffs. It wasn't pretty anymore. I looked down and saw the top of the Clusterous Forest, moving in slow ripples like spooky laundry hung out to dry, and the distant sight of the needles spilling ink into the waiting barrels.

Theodora braked and got out of the car, stretched, and took off her gloves and her leather helmet. I finally had a good look at her long, thick hair, which was almost as strange a sight as everything I had seen on the way. I needed a haircut, but S. Theodora Markson made me look bald. Her hair stretched out every which way from her head in long, curly rows, like a waterfall made from tangled yarn. It was very hard to listen to her while it was in front of me.

"Listen to me, Snicket," my chaperone said. "You are on probation. Your penchant for asking too many questions and for general rudeness makes me reluctant to keep you. 'Penchant' is a word which here means habit."

"I know what penchant means," I said.

"That is exactly what I'm talking about," Theodora said sternly, and quickly ran her fingers through her hair in an attempt to tame it. It was impossible to tame, like leeches. "Our first client lives here, and we are meeting with him for the first time. You are to speak as little as possible and let me do the work. I am very excellent at my job, and you will learn a great deal as long as you keep quiet and remember

you are merely an apprentice. Do you understand?"

I understood. Shortly before graduation
I'd been given a list of people with whom I
could apprentice, ranked by their success in
their various endeavors. There were fifty-two
chaperones on the list. S. Theodora Markson
was ranked fifty-second. She was wrong.
She was not excellent at her job, and this was
why I wanted to be her apprentice. The map
was not the territory. I had pictured working
as an apprentice in the city, where I would have
been able to complete a very important task
with someone I could absolutely trust. But the
world did not match the picture in my head,
and instead I was with a strange, uncombed
person, overlooking a sea without water and a
forest without trees.

I followed Theodora along the driveway and
up a long set of brick stairs to the front door,

where she rang the doorbell six times in a row. It felt like the wrong thing to do, standing at the wrong door in the wrong place. We did it anyway. Knowing that something is wrong and doing it anyway happens very often in life, and I doubt I will ever know why.

CHAPTER THREE

After the sixth ring of the doorbell, I could hear faint footsteps approaching the door, but my thoughts had drifted someplace else. Instead of standing at the door of a mansion in this strange, faraway place, I imagined myself back in the city, standing at the top of a hole with my tape measure and my trusted associate. I pictured myself in possession of all the belongings I had put in my suitcase. I pretended that I had no need of a strange, shiny mask. And most of all I had a vision of myself in which I was not so very hungry. I had planned to eat something on the train but instead had journeyed a great distance in Theodora's roadster with not even the tiniest of snacks, and while in my mind I was quite full from an excellent meal, in Stain'd-by-the-Sea my stomach was growling something awful.

It was for this reason that I took little notice of the butler who opened the door for us or the hallway he led us down before opening a set of double doors and asking us to wait in the library. I should have paid attention. An apprentice should pay close attention to the details of a new location, particularly if the furniture seems wrong for the room, or if the library seems to have only a handful of books in it. But I didn't even look back as the butler shut the doors behind us, and instead cast my eyes across the large, dim room to a small, bright table where tea had been laid out on a tray, along with a dozen cookies on a plate. I walked over to get a closer look. They were almond cookies, although they could have been made of spinach and shoes for all I cared. I ate eleven of them, right in a row. It is rude to take the last cookie.

Theodora had sat down on a small sofa and was looking at me with disgust. "Not proper, Snicket," she said, shaking her head. "Not proper at all."

"I saved you one," I said.

"Sit right here next to me and stop talking," Theodora said, tapping the sofa with a glove. "The butler told us to wait, and wait we shall."

Wait we did. We waited long enough that I looked for something to read. The few books on the shelves looked like the sort of books someone would leave behind rather than ever look at again. I read five chapters of a book about a boy named Johnny. He lived in America when America was still England. One day he burned his hand and was no longer able to work as a silversmith, which sounded like a miserable line of work anyway, so he took an interest in local politics. I felt sorry for the guy, but I had other things on my mind and put the book back on the shelf just as the double doors opened and an old woman walked into the room with a limp and a black cane to go with it.

"Thank you for waiting," she said in a voice even creakier than I'd thought it would be. "I am Mrs. Murphy Sallis."

"S. Theodora Markson," said S. Theodora Markson, standing up quickly and yanking me up beside her. "I had been told that my client was a man."

"I am not a man," said the woman, with a frown.

"I can see that," Theodora said.

"It's very nice to meet you," I said quickly.

Theodora glared at me, but Mrs. Murphy Sallis gave me a brief smile and offered me her hand, which was as smooth and soft as old lettuce.

"Charming boy," she said, and then frowned again at Theodora. "What does the *S* stand for?"

"Standing next to me is my apprentice," Theodora said, and handed the old woman an envelope. Mrs. Sallis tore it open and lowered herself into the largest chair to read it, without offering to ring for more cookies. Even in the dim room, I could see the insignia on the letter, which matched that of my letter of introduction. I've never cared for it. The old woman looked about as interested in the letter as I was in Johnny's silversmithing. "This will do," she said, and put the letter down on the tray with a quick look at the crumb-covered plate. Then, with a great sigh, as if preparing herself for an important performance, Mrs. Sallis looked at Theodora and began to speak.

"I'm in desperate need of your assistance,"

she began. "A priceless item has been stolen from my home, and I need to get it back."

"First," Theodora said, "we'll need to know what the item is."

"I know that," the woman snapped. "I was just about to tell you. It's a small statue, about the size of a bottle of milk. It's made of an extremely rare species of wood that is very shiny and black in color. The statue has been in my family for generations and has been valued at upward of a great deal of money."

"A great deal of money," Theodora repeated thoughtfully. "When was it stolen?"

"That I do not know," Mrs. Sallis said. "I have not been in this room for quite some time, and normally the statue is kept here in the library, on the mantel over there."

We looked at the mantel. Sure enough, there was nothing on it.

"Two days ago I came in here looking for

something and saw that it was missing. I've been upset ever since."

"Hmm," Theodora said, and walked quickly to the windows of the library, which were shrouded by heavy curtains. She yanked them aside and then fiddled with both of the windows, first one and then the other. "These are latched."

"They're always latched," Mrs. Sallis replied.

"Hmm." Theodora crossed slowly to the mantel and then leaned her head down to look at it very closely. There was still nothing on it. She took two large, slow steps backward and then stared up at the ceiling. "What is above this room?"

"A small parlor, I believe," the old woman said.

"The burglar could have broken into this room from the parlor," Theodora said. "He or she would have had to saw a hole in the ceiling, of course, but then gravity would have done the rest, dropping the burglar right in front of the mantel."

Everyone in the room looked at the ceiling, which was as red and blank as the surface of an apple.

"Glue," Theodora said. "Glue and plaster could cover it up."

The old woman put her hand to her head. "I know who stole it," she said.

Theodora coughed a little. "Well, that doesn't necessarily mean they didn't come in through the ceiling."

"Who stole it?" I asked.

The old woman rose and limped to one of the windows. She pointed out at the lighthouse we had passed on the way. "The Mallahan family," she said. "They've been enemies of my family for many lifetimes. They always swore they'd steal the statue, and at last they have."

"Why didn't you call the police?" I asked.

Mrs. Murphy Sallis looked surprised and stammered for a few seconds before Theodora butted in. "Because she called us," she said. "Rest assured, Mrs. Sallis, we will find this statue and bring the thieves to justice."

"I just want the statue back with its rightful owner," the old woman said hastily. "I want nobody to know you are working for me, and I want nothing done to the Mallahans. They're nice people."

It is not common to hear someone refer to enemies of their family for many lifetimes as "nice people," but Theodora nodded and said, "I understand."

"Do you?" the woman demanded. "Do you promise to return the statue to its rightful owner, and do you promise to be discreet about the Sallis name?"

My chaperone waved her hand quickly, as

if an insect were flying in her face. "Yes, yes, of course."

Mrs. Sallis turned her gaze to me. "And what about you, lad? Do you promise?"

I looked right back at her. To me, a promise is not an insect in my face. It is a promise. "Yes," I said. "I promise to return the statue to its rightful owner, and I promise to be discreet about who has hired us."

"Mrs. Sallis has hired *me*," Theodora said sternly. "You're just my apprentice. Well, Mrs. Sallis, I believe we're all done here."

"Perhaps Mrs. Sallis could tell us what the statue looks like," I said.

"I'm sorry," Theodora said to Mrs. Sallis. "My apprentice apparently wasn't listening. But I remember. It's the size of a milk bottle, made of shiny, black wood."

"But what is it a statue of?"

Mrs. Murphy Sallis limped one step closer and

gave us each a long, dark look. "The Bombinating Beast," she said. "It is a mythical creature, something like a sea horse. Its head looks like this."

She lifted one limp hand from her cane to reveal the head of a creature carved into its top. The creature looked like a sea horse like a hawk looks like a chicken. Its eyes were thin and fierce, and its lips were drawn back in a snarl to reveal rows and rows of tiny, sharp teeth. Even at the end of a cane, it looked like something you'd want to avoid, but plenty of people put nasty things on their mantels.

"Thank you," Theodora said briskly. "You'll be hearing from us, Mrs. Sallis. We'll let ourselves out."

"Thank you," the old woman said, and took another deep sigh as we walked back down the hallway and out of the mansion. The butler was standing on the lawn, facing away from us with a bowl of seeds he was throwing to some noisy birds. They whistled to him, and he whistled back, mimicking their calls exactly. It would have been pleasant to watch that for a few more minutes, and I wish I had. But instead Theodora started the roadster's engine, put her helmet back on her head, and was halfway down the driveway before I had time to shut the door.

"This will be an easy case!" she crowed happily. "It's not often that a client gives us the name of the criminal. You're bringing me luck, Snicket."

"If Mrs. Sallis knew who the burglar was," I asked, "why wouldn't she call the police?"

"That's not important," Theodora said. "What we need to figure out is how the Mallahans broke in through the ceiling."

"We don't know that they broke in through the ceiling," I said.

"The windows were latched," Theodora said.

46

"There's no other way they could have gotten into the library."

"We got in through a pair of double doors," I said, but Theodora just shook her head at me and kept driving. We passed the small white cottage and then came to a stop in front of the lighthouse, which needed painting and seemed to lean ever so slightly to one side.

"Listen, Snicket," she said, taking off her helmet again. "We can't just knock on the door of a house of thieves and tell them we're looking for stolen goods. We're going to have to use a con, a word which here means a bit of trickery. And don't tell me you already know what that means. In fact, don't say anything at all. You hear me, Snicket?"

I heard her, so I didn't say anything at all. She marched up to the door of the lighthouse and rang the doorbell six times.

"Why do you always—"

"I said *don't say anything*," Theodora hissed as the door swung open. A man stood there wearing a bathrobe and a pair of slippers and a large, yawning mouth. He looked like he was planning on staying in that bathrobe for quite some time.

"Yes?" he said when the yawn was done with him.

"Mr. Mallahan?" Theodora asked.

"That's me."

"You don't know me," she said in a bright, false voice. "I'm a young woman and this is my husband and we're on our honeymoon and we're both crazy about lighthouses. Can we come in and talk to you for a minute?"

Mallahan scratched his head. I started to hide my hands behind my back, because I wasn't wearing a wedding ring, but it occurred to me that there were lots of reasons not to believe that a boy of almost thirteen was married to a woman of Theodora's age, so I left my hands where they were. "I guess so," the man said, and ushered us into a small room with a large, winding staircase leading up. The staircase undoubtedly led to the top of the lighthouse, but to get there, you would have had to step over the girl sitting on the stairs with a typewriter. She looked about my age, although the typewriter looked a lot older. She pecked a few sentences into it and then paused to look up at me and smile. Her smile was nice to look at, along with the hat she was wearing, which was brown with a rounded top like a lowercase *a*. She looked up from her typing, and I saw that her eyes were full of questions. "I was just trying to find the coffee," Mallahan said, gesturing to an open door through which I could see a small kitchen stacked with dishes. "Do you want some?"

"No," Theodora said, "but I'll come along

and talk to you while we let the children play."

Mallahan gave a shrug and walked off to the kitchen while Theodora made little shooing motions at me. It is always terrible to be told to go play with people one doesn't know, but I climbed the stairs until I was standing in front of the typing girl.

"I'm Lemony Snicket," I said.

She stopped typing and reached into the band of her hat for a small card, which she gave me to read.

MOXIE MALLAHAN. THE NEWS.

"*The News*," I repeated. "What's the news, Moxie?"

"That's what I'm trying to find out," she replied, and typed a few more words. "Who's that woman who knocked on the door? How could she be married to you? Where did you come from? What makes you crazy about lighthouses? Why did she shoo you away? And is *Snicket* spelled like it sounds?"

"Yes," I said, answering the last question first. "Are you a reporter?"

"I'm the only reporter left in Stain'd-by-the-Sea," Moxie replied. "It's in my blood. My parents were both reporters when this place wasn't just a lighthouse but a newspaper, too. *The Stain'd Lighthouse.* Maybe you've heard of it?"

"I can't say I have," I said, "but I'm not from around here."

"Well, the newspaper's out of business," Moxie said, "but I still try to find out everything that's happening in this town. So?"

"So?"

"So what's happening, Snicket? Tell me what's going on."

She put her fingers down on the keys, ready

to type whatever I was going to say. Her fingers looked ready to work.

"Do you generally know everything that's happening in this town?" I asked.

"Of course," she said.

"Really, Moxie?"

"Really, Snicket. Tell me what's going on and maybe I can help you."

I stopped looking at her typewriter and looked at her eyes. Their color was pretty interesting, too—a dark gray, like they'd once been black but somebody had washed them or perhaps had made her cry for a long time. "Can I tell you without you writing it down?" I asked.

"Off the record, you mean?"

"Off the record, yes."

She reached under the typewriter and clicked something, and the whole apparatus folded into a square with a handle, like a black metal suitcase. It was a neat trick. "What is it?"

I looked back down the stairs to make sure nobody else was listening. "I'm trying to solve a mystery," I said, "concerning the Bombinating Beast."

"The mythical creature?"

"No, a statue of it."

"That old gimcrack?" she said with a laugh. "Come on up."

She stood and ran quickly up the spiral staircase, her shoes making the sort of racket that might give your mother a headache, if you have that sort of mother. I followed her up a few curves to a large room with high ceilings and piles of junk that were almost as high. There were a few large, dusty machines with cobwebbed cranks and buttons that hadn't been pressed for years. There were tables with chairs stacked on them, and piles of paper shoved underneath desks. You could tell it had been a busy room once, but now Moxie and I were the only people in it, and all that busyness was just a ghost.

"This is the newsroom," she said. "*The Stain'd Lighthouse* was here on the waterfront, typing up stories day and night, and this was the center of the whole operation. We'd develop photographs in the basement, and reporters would type up stories in the lantern room. We'd print the paper with ink made just that day, and we'd let the papers dry on the long hawser that runs right out the window."

"Hawser?" I said, and she clomped to the window and opened it. Outside, hanging high over the trees, was a long, thick cable that ran straight down the hill toward the gleaming windows of the mansion I'd just visited.

"It looks like that goes right down to the Sallis place," I said.

"The Mallahans and the Sallises have been friends for generations," Moxie said. "We got our water from the well on their property, and our science and garden reporters did research on their grounds. Our copy editor rented their guest cottage, and we would turn on the lighthouse lantern for midnight badminton parties. Of course, all that's gone now."

"Why?"

"Not enough ink," Moxie said. "The industry is down to its last few schools of octopi. This whole town is fading, Snicket. There's a library, and a police station, and a few other places open for business, but more than half of the buildings in town are completely unpeopled. *The Stain'd Lighthouse* had to shut down publication. Most inkworkers have been fired. The train passes through about once a month. Soon Stain'd-by-the-Sea will be gone completely. My mother got a letter from the city and left for a job with another newspaper."

"When are you joining her?" I asked.

Moxie looked quietly out the window for

a moment, giving me an idea about who had made her cry. "As soon as I can," she said with a sigh, and I realized it had been the wrong thing to say.

"The Bombinating Beast," I reminded her.

"Oh, right," she said, and walked over to a table covered in a sheet. "The Bombinating Beast was sort of the mascot of the newspaper. Its body made the *S* in *Stain'd*. Legend has it that hundreds of years ago Lady Mallahan slew the Bombinating Beast on one of her voyages. So my family has quite the collection of Bombinating merchandise, although no one's ever cared about it except—"

"Snicket!" Theodora's voice came from the bottom of the staircase. "Time to go!"

"Just one minute!" I called back.

"Right this minute, Snicket!" Theodora answered, but I didn't leave right that minute. I stayed as Moxie drew back the sheet to reveal another table piled with items nobody

wanted. The sea horse face of the Bombinating Beast wasn't any less hideous no matter how many times I saw it. There were three stuffed Bombinating Beasts that you might give to a baby you wanted to frighten, and a deck of cards with Bombinating Beasts printed on the back. There were Bombinating Beast coffee mugs and Bombinating Beast cereal bowls stacked up with Bombinating Beast napkins on Bombinating Beast place mats. But beside this beastly meal, next to the Bombinating Beast ashtray and the Bombinating Beast candleholders, was an object very shiny and black in color. Moxie had called it a gimcrack, and Mrs. Murphy Sallis had called it a priceless item. It was about the size of a bottle of milk and said to be valued at upward of a great deal of money. It was the Bombinating Beast, the statue we were looking for, as dusty and forgotten as the rest of the items in the room.

"Snicket!" Theodora called again, but I didn't

answer her. I spoke to the statue instead. "Hello," I said. "What are you doing here?"

Moxie looked at me and smiled. "I guess your mystery is solved, Snicket," she said, but that, too, was the wrong thing to say.

CHAPTER FOUR

"While you were mucking about with that flatfooted girl," Theodora said to me as she started her roadster and put on her helmet, "I managed to solve the mystery. I have reason to believe that the Bombinating Beast is in that very lighthouse."

"It is," I said.

"Then we're in agreement," Theodora said. "I had quite a talk with that Mr. Mallahan. He told me he used to work in the newspaper business but lately has had quite the run of bad luck! *Aha!*"

My chaperone looked at me like I should *aha!* back, but all I could manage was a quiet "ah." I made a note to *ha* later. We drove past the mansion toward the center of town. Moxie was right. It was an unpeopled place. Stain'd-by-the-Sea looked like it had been a regular town once, with shops full of items, and restaurants full of food, and citizens looking for one or the other. But now the whole place had faded to gray. Many of the buildings had windows that were broken or boarded up, and the sidewalks were uncared for, with great cracks in the concrete, and empty bottles and cans rolling around in the bored wind. Whole blocks were completely empty, with no cars except our own and not a single pedestrian on the streets. Some ways away was a building shaped like a pen that towered over the rest of the town, as if Stain'd-by-the-Sea were about to be crossed out. I didn't like it. It looked like anyone could move in and do anything they wanted without anyone stopping them. The Clusterous Forest almost looked friendlier.

"No job, no wife, a man like that can get desperate," Theodora was saying. "Desperate enough to steal a very valuable statue from one of his enemies. When I asked him if there was anything in his house that was worth upward of a great deal of money, he looked at me strangely and said something about his only daughter. I think he has it hidden away somewhere."

"It's upstairs," I said, "on a table covered in a sheet."

"What?" Theodora stopped at a red light. I had seen no other cars on the road. Only the stoplights were around, telling nobody but us when to stop and when to go. "How did you find it?"

"His daughter showed me," I said. "She's

not flatfooted, by the way. She just wears heavy shoes."

"Be sensible," Theodora said. "How did you get her to show it to you?"

"I asked her," I said.

"She must be onto us," Theodora said, with a frown. "We'd better act quickly if we want to steal it back."

"How do we even know it was stolen?" I asked.

"Don't be a numbskull, Snicket. Mrs. Sallis told us it was stolen right off her mantel."

"Moxie said the statue belonged to her family. The beast was the mascot of *The Stain'd Lighthouse.*"

"That lighthouse wasn't stained. It just needed painting."

"We need to investigate further," I said.

"No, we don't," Theodora said firmly. "We're not going to call a distinguished woman a liar and believe the word of a little girl. Particularly one with a ridiculous name."

"That reminds me," I said. "What does the *S* stand for?"

"Silly boy," she said with a shake of her head, and pulled the car to a stop. We were parked in front of a building with a sagging roof and a porch crowded with dying plants in cracked flowerpots. A painted wooden sign, which must have been magnificent to look at centuries ago when it was painted, read THE LOST ARMS. "This is our headquarters," Theodora said, taking off her helmet and shaking her hair. "This is our lodgings and our nerve center and our home office and our command post. This is where we'll be staying. Carry the suitcases, Snicket."

She bounded up the stairs, and I got out of the roadster and looked around the dreary street. Down the block I could see one other open business, a lonely-looking restaurant called

Hungry's, and in the other direction the street came to a dead end at a tall building with gray carved pillars on either side of the doors. There was no one about, and the only other car I could see was a dented yellow taxi parked in front of the restaurant. I was hungry again, or maybe I was still hungry. Something in me felt empty, certainly, but the more I stood there the less sure I was that it was my stomach, so I leaned into the backseat and pulled out two suitcases— the one that Theodora had said was mine and another, larger one that must have been hers. It was burdensome to carry them up the stairs, and when I entered the Lost Arms, I put them down for a minute to catch my breath in the lobby.

The room had a complicated smell, as if many people were in it, but there were very few things in the place. There was a small sofa with a table next to it that was even smaller, and it was hard to say from this angle which was grimier.

It was probably a tie. On the table was a small wooden bowl of peanuts that were either salted or dusty. There was a small booth in the corner, where a tall man with no hat was talking on the phone, which I looked at wistfully for a moment, hoping he would hang up and give me a chance to use it. There was a desk in a far corner, where Theodora was talking to a thin man who was rubbing his hands together, and right in the center of the room was a tall statue made of plaster, of a woman who wore no clothes and had no arms.

"I guess you have it worse than I do," I said to her.

"Stop dawdling, Snicket," Theodora called to me, and I trudged our suitcases to the desk. The thin man was handing two keys to Theodora, who handed me one of them.

"Welcome to the Lost Arms," the man said in a voice as thin as he was. His manner reminded me of a word I'd been taught and then had forgotten. It was on the tip of my tongue, as was one last cookie crumb. "I'm the owner and operator of this establishment, Prosper Lost. You can call me Prosper, and you can call me anytime you have a problem. The phone is right over there."

"Thank you," I said, thinking I'd probably just walk over to the desk rather than wait for the phone.

"As you requested," Prosper continued, "I've arranged for you two to have the least expensive room, the Far East Suite, located on the second floor. I'm afraid the elevator isn't working today, so you'll have to take the stairs. May I ask how long you plan on staying?"

"For the duration," my chaperone said, and walked quickly toward a carpeted staircase with banisters that looked too fragile to touch. I did not need Theodora or anyone else to explain that "for the duration" was a phrase which here meant nothing at all. Instead, I followed Theodora up the stairs, dragging the suitcases behind me, and down a narrow hallway to a room marked FAR EAST SUITE. Theodora got the key into a fight with the keyhole, but after a few minutes the door was open, and we stepped into our new home.

You've probably never been to the Far East Suite at the Lost Arms in Stain'd-by-the-Sea, but I'm sure you've been in a room you couldn't wait to leave, which is about the same thing. Most of the room was a large bed and a small bed, separated by a squat chest of drawers that appeared to be frowning. There was a door to a bathroom, and a small table in a corner with a metal plate that plugged into the wall, probably for heating up food. Overhead was a light fixture shaped like a complicated star, and the only thing on the walls was a painting, hung over the smaller bed, of a little girl holding a dog with a bandaged paw. The room was quite dark, but even when I unshuttered the lone window, the Far East Suite was no brighter than it had been.

"We're sharing a room?" I asked.

"Be sensible, Snicket," Theodora replied. "We can change our clothes in the bathroom. Now why don't you slide your suitcase under your bed and go out to the lobby to play or something? I'm going to unpack and take a nap. That always helps me think, and I need to think of how we can get our hands on that statue."

"There's a hawser," I said, "that runs from the lighthouse down to the Sallis mansion."

"Hawser?"

"A hawser is a cable," I said.

"I knew that."

"Really?" I couldn't help asking. "I had to learn it from a little girl."

Theodora sat on the large bed with a long sigh and ran her hands through her endless hair. "Let me rest, Snicket," she said. "Be back for dinner. I think we'll dine later this evening."

"Later than what?"

"Later than usual."

"We've never dined together."

"You're not helping me rest, Snicket."

I was restless, too, and slid my suitcase under the bed and walked out of the room, shutting the door behind me. A minute later I was back on the sidewalk, looking at the empty street with my hands full of peanuts I'd grabbed from the lobby. I had more privacy outside the Lost Arms than I did in the Far East Suite. I liked privacy, but I still didn't know how to fill the time I had before dinner, so I turned and walked down the block to the building with the pillars, which looked like my best bet for something interesting.

I used to be that young man, almost thirteen, walking alone down an empty street in a half-faded town. I used to be that person, eating stale peanuts and wondering about a strange, dusty item that was stolen or forgotten and that belonged to one family or another or their enemies or their friends. Before that I was a child receiving an unusual education, and before that I was a baby who, I'm told, liked looking in mirrors and sticking his toes into his mouth. I used to be that young man, and that child, and that baby, and the building I stood in front of used to be a city hall. Stretched out in front of me was my time as an adult, and then a skeleton, and then nothing except perhaps a few books on a few shelves.

And now stretched out in front of me was a scraggly lawn and a tall metal statue so worn from rain and age that I could not tell what it was a statue of, even when I was close enough to touch it. The shadows of the building's two pillars were wiggly stripes, and the building itself looked like it had been slapped several times by a giant creature that had lost its temper. The pillars held an arch with the words STAIN'D-BY-THE-SEA written in letters that had once been darker, and carved into the wall were the words CITY and HALL, although they were difficult to read, as someone had hurriedly nailed up two other signs on top of them. Over CITY was a sign that read POLICE STATION, and over HALL was a sign that read LIBRARY. I walked up the steps and made the sensible choice.

The library was one enormous room, with long, high metal shelves and the perfect quiet that libraries provide for anyone looking for an answer. A mystery is solved with a story. The story starts with a clue, but the trouble is that you usually have no idea what the clue is, even if you think you know. I thought the clue was the Bombinating Beast, sitting under a sheet in a forgotten room of a lighthouse, and I wondered how I might find out more. I crossed the room looking for the librarian, and soon found him behind a desk, swatting at a couple of moths with a checkered handkerchief. The moths were fluttering over a small sign at the desk that read DASHIELL QWERTY, SUB-LIBRARIAN. He was younger than I think of librarians as being, younger than the father of anyone I knew, and he had the hairstyle one gets if one is attacked by a scissors-carrying maniac and lives to tell the tale. He was wearing a black leather jacket with various metallic items up and down the sleeves, which jangled slightly as he went after the moths.

"Excuse me," I asked, "are you the librarian?"

Qwerty waved his handkerchief one more time at the moths and then gave up. "Sub-librarian," he said in a voice so deep I thought for a moment we were both at the bottom of a well. "Stain'd-by-the-Sea cannot afford a permanent librarian, so I am here instead."

"How long have you been here?"

"Since I replaced the other one," he said. "Can I help you?"

"I am looking for information on local legends," I said.

"Dame Sally Murphy is probably Stain'd-by-the-Sea's most famous actress," Qwerty suggested. "There should be a book about her career in the Theater Section."

"Not that kind of legend," I said. "I mean old stories about strange creatures."

Qwerty stepped around the desk. "Allow me to lead you to Mythology," he said, and without hesitating he walked me toward a row of shelves in the center of the room. "There's also a good Zoology and Oceanography Section, if you're interested in real animals."

"Not today, thank you."

"One never knows. They say in every library there is a single book that can answer the question that burns like a fire in the mind."

"Perhaps, but not today."

"Very well. Shall I help you further, or do you like to browse on your own?"

"Browse on my own, please," I said, and Qwerty nodded and walked away without another word. The Mythology Section had several books that looked interesting and one that looked like it would be helpful. Sadly, it was not one of the ones that looked interesting. I found a table in a far corner where I could read without being disturbed and opened *Stain'd Myths*.

According to chapter 7, the Bombinating Beast was a mythological creature, half horse and half shark—although some legends claim half alligator and half bear—that lurked in the waters just outside Stain'd-by-the-Sea. It had a great appetite for human flesh and made a terrifying bombinating sound—I had to get up from the table and find a dictionary to learn that "bombinating" was a word which here meant buzzing—when looking for prey. Moxie had struck me as a somewhat unusual girl but not a liar, and, sure enough, there was a story that Lady Mallahan had slain the Bombinating Beast hundreds of years ago, although the author said that in all likelihood Lady Mallahan had just found a dead walrus on the beach at the bottom of the lighthouse's cliffs, and the local townspeople gossiped about it until it became much more interesting. Other stories said that people could tame the Bombinating Beast by imitating its fearsome buzz, and there was a myth about a wizard who held the beast under his power, as long as the terrible monster was kept fed. In the olden days, a gong was rung in the town square to warn away the beast on moonless nights. The gong was long gone, but the legend lingered. Mothers still told their children and their husbands that the Bombinating Beast would eat them if they did not finish their vegetables, and locals still dressed as the Bombinating Beast on Halloween and

Purim, with masks that looked not very different from the one I'd donned in the roadster, at least in the book's illustrations. Supposedly sailors still saw the Bombinating Beast, swimming with its body curled up like an underwater question mark, although with the sea drained, I couldn't imagine that this could be true, at least not anymore.

The book did not say anything about a statue, valuable or otherwise, and so I stopped reading about the Bombinating Beast and got interested in the chapter about the Stain'd witches, who had ink instead of blood in their veins. I wondered what they kept in their pens.

I read for quite some time before I was distracted by a noise that sounded like a rock being thrown against the wall, just above my head. I looked up in time to see a small object fall to the table. It was a rock, which had been thrown against the wall, just above my head. It would be nice to think of something clever to say when something like that happens, but I always ended up saying the same thing.

"*Hey*," I said.

"*Hey*," repeated a mocking voice, and a boy about my age stuck his head out from behind a shelf. He looked like the child of a man and a log, with a big, thick neck and hair that looked like a bowl turned upside down. He had a slingshot tucked into his pocket and a nasty look tucked into his eyes.

"You almost hit me," I said.

"I'm trying to get better," he said, stepping closer. He wanted to tower over me, but he wasn't tall enough. "I can't be expected to hit my target every time."

"That's your idea of fun?" I said. "Slinging rocks at people in the library?"

"I prefer to hit birds," he said, "but there aren't very many birds around here anymore."

"I can't imagine why they wouldn't want to

be frolicking with a nice guy like you," I said.

"Hold still," the boy replied, taking out his slingshot. "Let me see if I can hit that idiotic smile of yours from across the room."

Qwerty appeared as if from nowhere. "*Stew,*" he said, a word that sounded much scarier in such a deep voice. "Leave this library at once."

"I'm allowed in here," Stew said, glaring at the librarian. "This is a public library."

"And you are a public nuisance," Qwerty replied, grabbing Stew's arm and propelling him toward the door. "Out."

"See you soon," Stew called out nastily to me, but he left without further insult, and Qwerty went over to examine the wall.

"I'm sorry about that," he said, frowning at a small dent and rubbing it with his finger. "Stew Mitchum is like something stuck at the bottom of a waste bin. I try and try to throw him out, but he just sticks there, getting older and older. Did you find what you were looking for?"

"Sort of," I said. "Can I check out books if I don't live in town?"

"Regrettably, no," Qwerty said. "But I open the library very early every day. You're always welcome to come in and read anything you like. It's not often we get people interested in theater."

I did not bother to remind him that famous actresses were not the legends I was researching. "Thank you," I said. "I suppose I should get going."

"Of course," Qwerty said, "if you have a library card, you can send requests for books from the library close to where you live."

"You mean, my library in the city can send books here that I can check out?"

"No," Qwerty said, "but you could fill out the paperwork here, and the book would be waiting for you in the city."

"I don't know when I'll be back there," I said. The city, and the people I liked best in it, seemed even farther away than they were.

Qwerty reached into a pocket of his jacket

and pulled out a blank card. "You see, how it works is that you write down your name and the title of the book, and the person working at the research desk sees what book you are requesting."

I thought quickly. "So the person at the research desk sees the title of the book I want?"

"Yes."

"Or their apprentice?"

"I suppose so," Qwerty said. "Have you changed your mind?"

"Yes," I said. "I'd like to request a book from the Fourier Branch."

"The Fourier Branch?" Qwerty repeated, taking a pencil from behind his ear. "Isn't that near where they're building that new statue?"

"I'm not sure," I said, perfectly sure.

"And what is your name?" he asked me.

I told him, and told him it was spelled like it sounded. He wrote it down in careful block letters and then paused with his pencil in the air.

"And the author of the book you're looking for?"

I was blank for a moment. "Sorry," I said.

"Sorry is the author's name?"

"Yes," I stammered. "I believe she's Belgian."

"Belgian," he said, and looked at me and wrote it down and looked at me again. "And the title of the book?" he said, and it was a perfectly reasonable question. I hoped my answer sounded reasonable, too.

"*But I Cannot Meet You at the Fountain*."

Qwerty looked at me, his face as blank as one of those extra pages tucked in the back of a book for notes or secrets. "So your complete request," he said, "is 'Sorry, *But I Cannot Meet You at the Fountain*.'"

"That's right," and Qwerty looked at me just for a second before slowly writing it down.

CHAPTER FIVE

I walked back to the Lost Arms feeling much lighter than I had all day. The library had been restorative, a word an associate of mine used to describe activities that clear the brain and make the heart happy. A root beer float is restorative, as is managing to open a locked door. Hopefully, I thought, this associate of mine would soon receive my request at the Fourier Branch of the library and save herself some trouble.

It was trouble that was waiting for me at

the Lost Arms, and one could spot it half a block away, as there was a car parked out front with a red light on top. It looked like a police car, but when I got closer, I saw it was a run-down station wagon with a flashlight taped to its roof. Nevertheless, there were two adults in uniform standing at the steps of the Lost Arms, where Theodora was sitting. She had to look up to speak to them, and her eyes looked serious and worried beneath her hair. As part of my education, I'd learned that one should never have a serious conversation in a position in which one has to look up at the other person. I'd thought this was a ridiculous thing to teach children, who tend to be shorter than anyone else, and said so. As punishment for speaking out in class, I had to sit in the corner. The teacher looked even taller from there.

"Snicket," Theodora said as I reached our hotel. "These are the Officers Mitchum."

The two officers turned to look at me, and

I found myself facing a man and a woman who looked so much alike they could only be twins or two people who had been married for a very long time. They both had pear-shaped bodies, with short, thick legs and grumpy-looking arms, and it looked like they had both tried on heads that were too small for them and were about to ask the head clerk for a larger size.

"My wife and I have questions for you," said the first Officer Mitchum, rather than "Hello" or "Nice to meet you" or "I thought you might be hungry, so I took the liberty of bringing you some lamb chops."

"Harvey," the other officer said sharply. "You're not supposed to call me your wife when we're on official business."

The first officer sighed. "Mimi, you're my wife whether we're on duty or not."

"Don't remind me," his wife replied. "I'm having a bad enough day as it is. It was your turn to empty the dishwasher, Harvey, but as usual you forgot, and I had to do it myself."

"Mimi, stop nagging me."

"I'm not nagging you."

"Yes you are."

"Harvey, gently pointing something out is not nagging."

"That was gentle? I've seen a pack of wolves act as gentle as that."

"When have you ever seen a pack of wolves?"

"Well, not actual wolves, but I've visited your sister's house, and her kids—"

I can't imagine there is anyone reading this who needs to be told that when two married adults start to argue, it can last for hours, if not days, and the only way to stop it is to interrupt them. "You said you had some questions for me?" I asked.

"We'll ask the questions around here," Mimi Mitchum said. "We're the law in Stain'd-by-the-Sea. We're the ones who catch criminals and put them on the train back to the city to be locked up. From the outskirts of town in the hinterlands to the boundary of the Clusterous Forest, we know every single thing that happens in this town. So when strangers arrive, we feel it is our duty to welcome them and ask them what exactly it is that they're doing here."

"We love ink," Theodora tried.

"You told Mr. Mallahan you loved light-houses."

"We love everything," Theodora said with a desperate smile.

"What my chaperone means," I said, "is that although we're here on business, we hope to take in some of the fantastic sights of this wonderful community. I was just admiring your police station, for instance."

"Harvey hung that sign himself," Mimi Mitchum said proudly.

"It's true," the male Officer Mitchum said, "but what we're here to say is that one sight we hope you will *not* enjoy is the inside of our only jail cell. We couldn't help but notice that soon after the arrival of two strangers, this town experienced a crime. It is a small crime, to be sure, but it is a crime nonetheless."

"What happened?" I asked.

"A streetlight was vandalized," Harvey Mitchum said. "Right around the corner from the library, someone slung a small rock and shattered the bulb. It's still too early to make assumptions, but it wouldn't be surprising if this crime could be traced to the two of you. Where have you been for the last hour, Snicket?"

"In the library," I answered.

"Can anyone verify this?"

"Dashiell Qwerty, the librarian."

"That ruffian," Mimi Mitchum scoffed. "I don't trust anyone who doesn't spend time on his appearance."

"I'd say he spent lots of time," I said. "That haircut looked like it took hours. He and I were interrupted by a young boy with a slingshot. Qwerty said his name was Stew."

The Officers Mitchum looked sternly at me, their mouths set in identical snarls. "Our son, Stewart," the female Mitchum said, "is a genius and a gentleman. He is certainly not a criminal. Why, he begged to come with us just in order to welcome you."

She gestured to the station wagon, and I saw for the first time Stew's thick, sneering head peering out the open window. When the eyes of the adults were upon him, he found an enormous smile someplace and plastered that on his face instead. "Nice to meet you, Lemony," he said to me in a falsely cheerful voice. "I love meeting nice people my own age! I do hope we become the bestest of friends!"

"You see?" Harvey Mitchum said to me as Stew stuck his tongue out at me without anyone seeing. "A charming boy."

"A *darling* boy," Mimi Mitchum said. "Lately

he's been interested in local bird life."

"I bet he grows up to be a brilliant scientist," her husband said.

"Or a doctor," said his wife.

"A *brilliant* doctor."

"Of course, Harvey. You know I meant a brilliant doctor. You don't have to embarrass me like that."

"I wasn't trying to embarrass you."

"Well, then you were wasting time."

"I wasn't wasting time! It only took a second!"

"Then what were you trying to do? Why would you even say such a thing if you weren't trying to embarrass your wife?"

"You said I shouldn't call you my wife when we're on duty!"

"And you said I was still your wife whether we were on duty or not."

"Excuse me," I said, "but if you don't have any more questions, I'd like to go to my room."

The Officers Mitchum looked at me in irritation for interrupting their argument. "We'll be keeping an eye on you two," Mimi Mitchum said, pointing a surprisingly long finger, and after a brief dispute over which Mitchum would drive, the station wagon rattled away down the street, and Theodora stood up to stare down at me.

"We're not in town one day," she said, "and already you're in trouble with the law. I'm disappointed in you, Snicket."

"I didn't vandalize a streetlight," I said.

"That's not important," she said with a shake of her hair. "We need to move tonight."

"Let's look for a place with two separate rooms."

"No, I mean tonight we must be interlopers," she said, "a word which here means stealing the Bombinating Beast and returning it to its rightful owners."

"I think the statue *is* with its rightful owners,"

93

I said, not adding that I had known what "inter-lopers" meant since I was ten years old and read a short story by a British man with a funny false name. "I did some research at the library, and local legends say that the Bombinating Beast has been associated with the Mallahan family for generations. And when Moxie Mallahan showed it to me, it looked very dusty, as if it hadn't been moved in years."

"Legends are just made-up stories," Theodora said scornfully, "and anyone can pour dust on something to make it look old. Some years ago I had a case where two brothers were arguing over a seashell collection. The younger brother poured dust on the shells to try to prove they were his, but I saw through his ridiculous ruse. In any case, it's all settled. I called the Sallis mansion this afternoon and made arrangements with the but-ler. We will take the statue from the lighthouse and climb out the window to reach the mansion by way of the hawser. The butler agreed to leave the window to the library open and signal us with a candle that all is clear. We will deliver the statue to him, and the case will be closed."

It struck me that it was probably not dust but sand on the shells, so that it was likely that the younger brother was the true owner of the sea-shell collection. It also struck me that it was not a good time to say this. My chaperone leaned in close to me. "What you are to do," she said, "is break into the lighthouse sometime this evening and wait inside. At midnight exactly you will open the door for me and lead me to the item in question. This must go off without a hitch, Snicket. People are watching us."

"You mean the Officers Mitchum?"

Theodora shook her head. "I mean someone from our organization. Wherever a chaperone goes, there is someone keeping an eye on things. You don't know this, Snicket, but out of fifty-two chaperones, I am ranked only tenth. If I solve this case quickly, my ranking will improve.

Now off you go. I'll see you at the lighthouse at midnight."

"What about dinner?" I asked.

"I already had dinner, thank you."

"What about *my* dinner?"

She frowned at me and walked up the stairs. "That's the wrong question, Snicket. There are more important things than dinner. Focus on the case."

I watched her go into the Lost Arms. It is true there are more important things than dinner, but it is difficult to keep those things in mind when you haven't had dinner. I allowed enough time for Theodora to reach her room, and then I walked into the Lost Arms myself, wondering who in this small, fading town could possibly be watching us. Prosper Lost was standing under the statue of the armless woman, an eager smile on his face. I remembered the word now that had been on the tip of my tongue. It was "obsequious," and it refers to people who behave like one's servants even when they aren't. It might sound like that would be pleasant, but it is not.

"Lovely evening, Mr. Snicket," he said to me.

"More or less," I agreed, looking across the lobby. Theodora had said she'd called the mansion, which meant the phone had not been in use. I hoped this was the case again, but a woman with a long fur stole around her neck was talking into it. "Is there another telephone anywhere nearby?" I asked.

Prosper Lost gave a small shrug. "Regrettably, no."

"Might you be able to give me a ride someplace?"

"Unregrettably, yes," Prosper said, "for a small fee, of course."

There may be a town in which lint in my pocket would count as a small fee, but I knew that Stain'd-by-the-Sea was not that town. I gave Prosper the sort of "Thank you" that does not mean "You have been very helpful" but means

"Please go away," and he did. I walked back out of the Lost Arms and stood out on the street wondering what to do, when a car pulled around the corner and stopped right in front of me. It was the dented yellow taxi I had seen earlier. Up close its dents looked worse, with one of the doors so banged up I could scarcely read the words BELLEROPHON TAXI printed on the side.

"Need a taxi, friend?" asked the driver, and it took me a moment to see that he was a little younger than I was. He had a friendly smile and a small scab on his cheek, like someone had given him a hard poke, and he was wearing a blue cap too large for him with BELLEROPHON TAXI printed on it in less dented lettering.

"I'm afraid I don't have any money," I said.

"Oh, that's OK," the boy replied. "With the way things are going in this town, we generally work just for tips."

"Do they let you drive at your age?" I asked.

"We're substituting for our father tonight," he replied. "He's sick."

"*We*? Who's *we*?"

The boy beckoned me over, and I leaned into the taxi and saw that he was sitting on a small pile of books to reach the steering wheel. Below him, crouched on the floor of the car, was a boy who looked a little younger, with his hands on the car's pedals. His smile was slightly wicked around the edges, as if he were the sort of person who occasionally poked his brother too hard.

"*We* is my brother and me," he said in a very high voice. "I'm Pecuchet Bellerophon, and he's my brother, Bouvard."

I told them my name and tried to pronounce theirs. "Nothing personal, but your names make my tongue tired. What do people call you?"

"They call me Pip," said the brother holding the steering wheel, "and him Squeak."

"Because I work the brakes," squeaked Squeak.

"Of course," I said. "Well, Pip and Squeak, I need to get to the lighthouse."

"The Mallahan place?" Pip said. "Sure, hop in."

I looked at the books he was sitting on. They looked like they were from the library, and some of them were books I admired very much. "Are you really sure you're old enough to drive?" I said.

"Are you old enough to go to the edge of town by yourself?" Pip replied. "Come on, get in."

I got in, and Squeak hit the gas. Pip steered the car expertly through the crumbly, half-deserted blocks of Stain'd-by-the-Sea. I spotted a grocery store, empty but open, and a department store with mannequins in the window that wanted to go home. The sun was beginning to set behind the tall tower in the shape of a pen. I tried to think about the statue of the Bombinating Beast, but my mind wandered, first to the caves I had seen, where frightened octopi were giving up their ink, and then to a bigger, deeper hole back in the city. I told myself to stop thinking about things I couldn't do anything about, and looked out the window as the taxi passed the Sallis mansion and continued on up the hill.

"Has your father ever driven Mrs. Sallis anyplace?" I asked.

"I don't think so," Pip replied. "When the Sallis family was in town, they had their own chauffeur."

"Aren't they in town now?"

"If they are, nobody told us," Squeak said from the floor of the car.

In a few minutes we had passed the small white cottage, and Squeak brought the taxi to an expert stop in front of the lighthouse door. "Do you want us to stick around and drive you back into town later?" Pip asked me.

"No, thanks," I said.

"Well, I hope you know what you're doing,

coming out here without a way to get back," Pip said, and reached around to open my door. "How about a tip?"

"Here's a tip," I said. "Next time you're at the library, check out a book about a champion of the world."

"By that author with all the chocolate?"

"Yes, but this one's even better. It has some very good chapters in it."

"That's the kind of tip we can use," Squeak said. "Pip reads to me between fares."

I shut the door behind me and gave the window of the cab a knock good-bye. Pip waved, and the taxi drove off. I waited until the sound of the engine had faded, and then stood for a moment looking up at the lighthouse. I hoped the same thing the two substitute drivers of Bellerophon Taxi hoped: that I knew what I was doing. I doubted it. I heard the eerie rustle of the wind through the seaweed of the Clusterous Forest, far below me, and then in front of me the more ordinary sound of a door opening.

"Lemony Snicket," said a voice.

I turned to look at the girl who had spoken. "What's the news, Moxie?"

"You tell me," she said. "You're the one who showed up at my door."

I squinted into the dim sky until I could see the faint, thick line of the hawser stretched out above me and angling down the hill. Why not, I thought, and turned back to Moxie Mallahan. "I'd like to extend an invitation," I said.

She gave me a small smile. "Oh yes? For what?"

"For a burglary taking place this evening at your home," I said, and walked through the door.

CHAPTER SIX

"That's a very kind invitation, Snicket," Moxie said to me, "but I'm not sure if it counts as a burglary if the item being stolen isn't treasured by its owner."

"What do you mean?" I asked her.

Moxie blinked at me under the brim of her hat. "You know what I mean, Snicket. You're here to steal the Bombinating Beast, aren't you?"

"How did you know?"

Moxie walked to her typewriter, which sat

in its usual spot on the stairway, with a sheet of paper still rolled into it. She scanned the paper to reread what she had typed earlier. "A stranger knocked on my door," she said, "with an older woman who briefly pretended to be his wife. The stranger asked to see a particular item and was clearly surprised that I showed it to him. And here you are, talking about burglary. So?"

"You're a very good journalist," I told her.

"Flattery bores me, Snicket. Are you here to steal the statue or not?"

"Yes," I decided to say. "Do you mind terribly?"

Her smile got quite a bit bigger. "Not at all," she said, and leaned against the open door of the lighthouse. She adjusted a knob on her typewriter and then looked me straight in the eye. She wasn't taller than I was, but I still had to look up to meet her gaze, as I had been taught never to do. "Lemony Snicket, I think it's time to tell me exactly what's going on."

"Are you really writing this up for the newspaper?" I asked. "I thought *The Stain'd Lighthouse* was out of business."

"I'm staying in practice as a journalist," she said. "Then when I leave this town, I'll be ready to join a newspaper."

"When your mother sends for you," I said.

"Stop stalling, Snicket. What exactly is going on?"

"There's someone who has taken an interest in the statue of the Bombinating Beast," I said, protecting the name of my client, as I had been requested to do. "This person has said that the statue is theirs and is worth upward of a great deal of money. I don't think that's true. I think the statue has been in your family for a very long time, since the days of Lady Mallahan, and I think that if it were very valuable, it wouldn't be covered in a sheet with a bunch of dusty, forgotten items. But it doesn't matter what I think. So I'm going to stay here until midnight, when my associate will arrive, and we will take the Bombinating Beast and escape down the hill on the hawser, and then my assignment will be over."

Moxie had been typing at a furious pace, but now she stopped and looked at me. "This person," she said, "who is interested in the Bombinating Beast—do they live here in Stain'd-by-the-Sea?"

"Yes," I said, incorrectly. "Why do you ask?"

Moxie walked across the room to a small desk and, with some difficulty, pulled open a drawer stuffed with papers. There is a drawer like this in every house in the world. She sifted through the papers with an expert eye and finally found what she was looking for. "Look at this thing," she said.

This thing was a telegram, dated six months before my graduation. It was addressed to Moxie's father, sent from a town I'd never heard of.

In the old code of telegram writing, the end of each sentence was marked with STOP, which made the message even more confusing than it already was.

GREETINGS SIR STOP
I AM VERY INTERESTED IN A CERTAIN
STATUE I BELIEVE IS IN YOUR
HOME STOP I BELIEVE IT IS CALLED
THE BOMBINATING BEAST STOP
IF YOU ARE WILLING TO SELL IT TO
ME I BELIEVE YOU WILL BE PLEASED
WITH THE PRICE I AM WILLING TO
PAY STOP PLEASE REPLY AT YOUR
EARLIEST CONVENIENCE STOP END
MESSAGE

"'I believe is in your home,'" I read out loud. "'I believe it is called the Bombinating Beast. I believe you will be pleased.' That's a lot of belief. What did your father reply?"

"My father never saw this telegram," Moxie said. "When it was sent, I'd already started handling all his correspondence."

"Well, did you reply?"

"I couldn't. Stain'd-by-the-Sea's only telegram dispatch closed its doors due to ink shortages, the day after this telegram arrived."

"So for all you know, this person has tried to send you many more telegrams."

"For all I know, yes."

"Did you investigate this at all?"

Moxie shook her head. "There wasn't much to investigate," she said. "The telegram is unsigned, and that town is quite a ways away. And, frankly, six months ago I had far more pressing matters than a statue nobody cares about."

I didn't press her about her pressing matters. "The writer of the telegram and the person who hired me might be the same person."

"Whoever they are," Moxie said, "they're welcome to that old thing. Nobody has to go to the trouble of burglary."

"Not according to my chaperone," I said.

"Well, in that case, what are we going to do until midnight?"

At last it was a question I could answer. "I was hoping we could have dinner," I said. "I've scarcely eaten today."

"I'm afraid I don't have much in the house," Moxie said. "My father said he was going to go to the market today, but he never got out of his robe. I'm afraid all we have is a great deal of wilted basil."

"Do you have a bulb of garlic, a lemon, a cup of walnuts, Parmesan cheese, pasta of some kind, and a fair amount of olive oil?"

"I think so," Moxie said, "although I think the cheese might be Asiago."

"Even better," I said, and I followed her

into the lighthouse's small kitchen, which was piled with dirty dishes and stacks of typewritten pages. Moxie cleared away the mess, and I put the walnuts in the oven to toast along with some peeled garlic coated in olive oil. I put a pot of water on to boil while Moxie looked in the fridge for something to drink. I was hoping for root beer, but all she could find was some cranberry juice, which tasted all right, but just all right. Together we plucked the leaves of the basil from the stems, grated the cheese, and squeezed the juice from the lemon, pausing to pick out the seeds with the tines of a fork decorated with an image of the Bombinating Beast. Then I put the pasta into the boiling water and mixed the remaining ingredients together, and soon we were sitting at the small wooden table, which wobbled slightly from a chipped leg, eating big bowls of orecchiette al pesto. It was just what I needed. I finished, wiped my mouth, and leaned back in my chair, which was just as wobbly.

Moxie finished her cranberry juice. "So?"

"Do you know," I asked her, "that *orecchiette* is Italian for 'little ears'? I know it's just the shape of the noodle, but some people don't like the idea of eating a big bowl of—"

"That's not what I mean, and you know it, Snicket. Why does someone want a statue everyone else has forgotten?"

"I wouldn't know," I said.

She reached over and opened up her typewriter to add a few sentences to her summary. "There's something going on that we can't see."

"That's usually the case," I said. "The map is not the territory."

"What does that mean?"

"It's an adult expression for the muddle we're in."

"Adults never tell children anything."

113

"Children never tell adults anything either," I said. "The children of this world and the adults of this world are in entirely separate boats and only drift near each other when we need a ride from someone or when someone needs us to wash our hands."

Moxie smiled at this and began to type. I meant to stack the dirty plates in the sink, but I liked staying at the table and watching her at work. "Do you like that?" I asked her. "Typing up what happens in the world?"

"Yes, I do," Moxie said. "Do you like what you do, Lemony Snicket?"

I stared out the kitchen's lone window. The moon had risen like a wide eye. "I do what I do," I said, "in order to do something else."

I was certain she would ask more questions, but we were interrupted by the lonely and familiar clanging of the bell. Moxie frowned at a clock with a face like that of an angry sea horse. "There's not usually an alarm at this hour," she said.

"When does it usually ring?"

"It depends. For a while it seemed like it was ringing less and less frequently, but lately it's started up again like gangbusters."

"Who rings it, anyway?"

Moxie stood on her chair to reach a high shelf. "The bell tower is over on Offshore Island, where there used to be a fancy boarding school that everyone called 'top drawer.'"

"I always thought that was a curious expression," I said. "After all, the most interesting things are usually in the bottom drawer."

Moxie smiled in agreement. "Back then the bell was rung by the student valedictorian, but Wade Academy closed some time ago. Now the bell is rung by someone from the Coast Guard, I think, or maybe it's the Octopus Council." She took two masks down from the shelf and handed one to me. "Don't worry, Snicket. We have plenty of spares. You won't get salt lung."

"Salt lung?"

"That's what the bell is for," she explained. "When the wind rises, it carries salt deposits left behind on the floor of the sea, which can be dangerous to breathe. The masks filter the salt out of the air."

"I heard the masks were for water pressure," I said.

Moxie frowned into her mask. "Where did you hear that?"

"From S. Theodora Markson," I said. "Where did you hear about salt lung?"

"Some society put out a pamphlet," Moxie said, gesturing to the stuffed drawer. We put on our masks and faced each other. "I don't much like talking with these on," she said. "Shall we read until we hear the all-clear?"

I gave her a masked nod of agreement, and

she led me into a small room where the walls were stuffed with bookshelves, and a large floor lamp stood in the middle. A big bulb cast a bright circle of light from under a shade decorated with a creature I was getting tired of looking at. There were two large chairs to sit in, one piled with more typewritten pages and the other surrounded by thick, sad-looking books on the decline of the newspaper industry and how to raise a daughter all by yourself. On the carpet I could see marks on the floor where a third chair had been dragged away. Moxie sat in her chair and put her typewritten notes in her lap and told me to help myself. I found a book that did nothing to relax my nerves. The story took place in some big woods where a little house was home to a medium-sized family who liked to make things. First they made maple syrup. Then they made butter. Then they made cheese, and I shut the book. It was more interesting to think about stealing a statue and making my way down a hill on a hawser high above the ground. "Interesting" is a word which here means that it made me nervous. I walked over to the window and tried to see how far it was from the lighthouse to the Sallis mansion, but the sun was long down, and outside was as black as the Bombinating Beast itself. It wasn't much of a view, but I stared at it for quite some time. After a while the bell clanged the all-clear from the island tower, and I took off my mask and realized Moxie had fallen asleep behind hers. I slipped her mask off and found a blanket to put on her and went back to my staring. I thought maybe if I stared hard enough, I could see the lights of the city I had left so very far behind. This was nonsense, of course, but there's nothing wrong with occasionally staring out the window and thinking nonsense, as long as the nonsense is yours.

Before long the clock was bombinating twelve times, but it was a quiet buzzing, so I heard Theodora's roadster outside without a problem. Moxie didn't stir, so I shook her shoulder slightly until her eyes flickered open.

"Is it time?" she said.

"It's time," I said, "but you would do me a great favor if you went to bed."

"And miss all the fun?" she said. "Not on your life, Lemony Snicket."

"You said yourself there's something going on we can't see," I said. "It might be something dangerous."

"In any case, it's something interesting," Moxie said, "and I'm going to find out all about it."

"Moxie, we can't burgle you if you're standing around watching. At least hide yourself."

She stood up. "Where?"

"You grew up in this lighthouse," I said. "You know all the best hiding places."

She nodded, packed up her typewriter, and walked out of the room. I put out the lights and then opened the front door. The roadster was parked in front of the lighthouse, but I couldn't see Theodora. I walked a few steps out and called her name.

My chaperone emerged from the night, crouching along the ground as she made her way. She had changed her clothes and was wearing black pants and a black turtleneck sweater, with black slippers on her feet and a small black mask over her eyes. Her immense hair was tied up in a complication of black ribbons, and her face was dusted with something black to help her blend in. I once saw a cat run up a chimney and then immediately come back down covered in soot to ruin the living room furniture, and I noticed several striking similarities between this memory and the woman who was moving stealthily toward me.

"There are burglary clothes in your suitcase,"

she hissed. "Why aren't you wearing them? We don't want to attract attention."

"Perhaps you should have parked someplace else," I said, pointing to the roadster.

"Keep your voice down," she said. "We'll wake people up."

One way to keep one's voice down is to stop talking altogether, which is also one way not to argue with somebody. I beckoned to Theodora, and we slipped into the house and made our way up the spiral staircase, Theodora pressing herself against the walls of the lighthouse and swiveling her head this way and that, and me walking like a normal person. I led her into the newsroom, removed the sheet, and pointed to the statue of the Bombinating Beast. She gestured to me that I should be the one to take it. I gestured back that she was the chaperone and the leader of this caper. She gestured to me that I shouldn't argue with her. I gestured to her that I was the one who had gotten us into the house in the first place. She gestured to me that my predecessor knew that the apprentice should never argue with the chaperone or complain and that I might model my own behavior after his. I gestured to her asking what the *S* stood for in her name, and she replied with a very rude gesture, and I grabbed the statue and tucked it into my vest. It was lighter than I thought it would be, and I felt less like a burglar and more like someone who was simply carrying an object from one place to another.

I opened the window and reached a hand down into the darkness until I could feel the hawser rough and cold against my palm. This made me feel more like a burglar. I held it steady for Theodora to grab with both hands, and then I lowered myself after her. I couldn't reach to shut the window, but I figured Moxie would do it once she came out of hiding. I wondered if she could see us now as we began to climb, hand over hand, along the hawser toward the Sallis

mansion at the bottom of the hill. We must have been strange shadows against the round, white moon. The rustling of the Clusterous Forest grew softer as we got farther and farther away, and the still night air filled my throat. I was not as high up as I thought I would be, and the hawser stayed steady as we continued our descent. In the moonlight I could see the trees below us, the thin branches all folded together like laced-up shoes, and the leaves looking lonely and uncomfortable. I could see the small white cottage, with something glinting in one of its windows—some small object that was reflecting the light of the moon. What I did not see was a candle, as Theodora had told me there would be, to signal that all was clear.

"Snicket," Theodora said, "this would be a good time to ask me a question."

"Why?" I tried.

"Because I am somewhat afraid of heights," she answered, "and answering an apprentice's questions would be a good way to distract me."

"OK," I said, and thought for a moment. "Do you think this is the way the statue was stolen?"

"Absolutely," Theodora said. "The Mallahans must have climbed down the hawser, grabbed the statue, and gone back out the way they came."

"I thought you said they came in from the parlor," I said, "by sawing a hole in the ceiling and letting gravity do the rest."

"That was an early theory of mine, yes," Theodora said, "but at least I was half-right: Gravity is involved. This would be a much harder climb if we were going up this hill instead of down."

What Theodora said was true—it would have been much harder to move hand over hand up the cable—but she had also said the thieves had gone back out the way they had come. Arguing with my chaperone, however, probably would not have distracted her from her condition. There was a word for a fear of heights, I knew, but I couldn't think of it. Something-phobia. "How do you think the thieves got into the Sallis mansion?" I asked.

"Through one of the windows of the library, of course," Theodora said. "The hawser goes right there."

"Mrs. Sallis said the windows are always latched," I reminded her.

"Well, they're not latched now," Theodora said. "Look. The butler is giving us the signal that all is clear."

Sure enough, I could see the faint shape of the open window, right where the hawser ended, and in the middle of that shape was a faint light. Hydrophobia? I thought. No, Snicket. That's the fear of water. The light did not look like a candle, as it was not flickering, and it was bright red in color. A bright red light reminded me of something that I also could not quite remember. Agoraphobia, I thought. No, Snicket. That's the fear of wide-open spaces.

"We're almost there," Theodora said. "In a minute the Bombinating Beast will be returned to its rightful owner, and this case will be closed."

I did not answer, because it had come to me all at once, like a light turning on. It was the red flashlight the Officers Mitchum had on top of their car. And "acrophobia" is the word for a fear of heights. I let go of the hawser and fell straight down into the trees.

CHAPTER SEVEN

It was pitch-black everywhere around me, and I felt as if I had fallen into the path of an enormous shadow. I had learned how to do it, in what you would probably call an exercise class, but that doesn't mean it wasn't difficult or frightening to fall that way. It was difficult and frightening. The fall was quick and dark, and I landed in the tree on my back, with many twigs and leaves poking at me in annoyance. Still I felt it. Then I relaxed, as I had been trained to do, and lay out on the top of the tree, letting it support my weight, but still I felt the enormous shadow cast upon me. It was not the shadow of the hawser, or of any of the other trees nearby. It was the face that appeared next to me, the face of a girl about my age. I could also see her hands, clutching the top of a ladder she must have leaned against the tree. Somehow I knew, as she blinked at me on top of the ladder, that the girl in question had already begun to cast an enormous shadow across my life and times.

"That was quite a stunt," she said. "Where did you learn to fall into a tree like that?"

"I've had an unusual education," I said.

"Did they teach you how to get down?"

"The best way is to wait for someone with a ladder."

"Someone?" she repeated. "Who, exactly?"

"I don't know," I said. "I don't know her name."

"Hello," she said, "I'm Ellington Feint," and I sat up to get a better look at her. It was not so dark that I couldn't see her strange, curved eyebrows, each one coiled over like a question mark. Green eyes she had, and hair so black it made the night look pale. She had long fingers, with nails just as black, and they poked out of a black shirt with long, smooth sleeves. And right before she started climbing down the ladder, I saw her smile, shadowy in the moonlight. It was a smile that might have meant anything. She was a little older than me, or maybe just a little taller. I followed her down.

When I reached the ground, Ellington Feint looked me over and then brushed a few leaves from my collar before offering her hand. The statue felt solid against my chest, and my hands were a little raw from the hawser. I could not see Theodora above me. It was possible she did not even know I was no longer behind her. "You haven't told me your name," Ellington said.

I shook her hand and told her.

"Lemony Snicket," she repeated. "Well, follow

me, Mr. Snicket. I live in that white cottage you passed over. You can rest there from your flight."

She led the way through the trees to the cottage I had seen from the road and from the hawser. Curiously, it looked even smaller now that we were close up, with a few windows here and there and a creaky-looking door and a white brick chimney puffing gray smoke into the night. A small arch over the door read HANDKERCHIEF HEIGHTS in faded letters. "They say a washerwoman used to live here," Ellington said when she saw me looking at the sign. "She used to hang handkerchiefs out to dry in the backyard, and that gave the cottage its name."

"Who lives here now?" I asked.

"Just me," she said, and opened the door. The cottage was no more than one small room, and most of that room appeared to be a fireplace with a colorful fire lighting every corner. The crackles of the fire mixed with music in the room, music I'd never heard and liked very much. There was a small cot in the far corner, with some rumpled blankets and pillows, and a large striped suitcase open on the floor, with all sorts of clothing tossed all sorts of ways. I spotted a long, fancy evening gown, some heavy hiking boots, an apron that a chef might wear, a red wig, a long, zippered green tube that might have been a purse, and two small hats I'd seen on the heads of Frenchmen in old photographs, both dirty, both worn, and both the color of a raspberry. In the opposite corner were a small sink and a short wooden table, completely bare, with one stool tucked under it. Sitting on a windowsill was a dented pair of binoculars, and on the floor in the center of the room was a small box with a crank on its side and a funnel on top. It took me a moment to realize that it was an old-fashioned record player, with the music I had never heard before winding out of the funnel. The music sounded interesting and complicated, and I wanted to ask the name of the tune. There were no books in the room as far as I could see. I should have known better.

"Have a seat," Ellington said to me, gesturing to the stool. "I'll make us some coffee. That should be restorative."

"*Coffee*?" I said, my voice louder and higher than I had planned. "I don't drink coffee."

"What do you drink?"

"Water," I said. "Tea. Milk sometimes. Orange juice in the morning. Root beer if I can find it."

"But not coffee?"

"People our age don't usually drink coffee," I said.

"Nor do they usually drop into trees," Ellington said. "I guess we've both had unusual educations."

I pulled out the stool and sat down, and Ellington busied herself at the sink with a metal coffeepot, rinsing it out and then filling it with water before adding several scoops of ground coffee from a paper bag stenciled with the shadow of a black cat. "Black Cat Coffee," she told me. "Corner of Caravan and Parfait. It's one of the last businesses left in Stain'd-by-the-Sea, and one of the only reasons I venture into town at all." She sighed. "Mostly I stay right here."

"And what do you do here?" I asked.

She gave me a small smile. "You first," she said. "Why are you flying through the air in the middle of the night?"

I reached into my vest and put down the Bombinating Beast on the table, a little too hard so it made a loud *thunk*. Ellington glanced at it briefly and then reached for a pair of creaky iron tongs, used for moving burning logs around in a fireplace. She used the tongs to pick up the coffeepot and then held it over the flames before looking back at me.

"What is that?" she asked. "Some kind of toy?"

I took a long, close look at the statue for the

first time. The Bombinating Beast still looked like a sea horse, if a sea horse could be a nasty, frightening animal. The eyes of the statue were actually small holes, as was the mouth, with its lips drawn back and the tiny, sharp teeth making thin lines over the hole. The entire statue was hollow, I realized, and for a moment I wondered if it had been carved to fit over a candle, so that the fire might shine through the eyes and mouth to create an eerie effect. I turned it over to look at the base of the statue, which had a strange slit cut into the wood. There was a small, thick piece of paper pasted over the slit like a patch. The paper patch felt curious to the touch, like the paper wrappings on cookies in the bakery. I shook the statue to see if there was anything inside, but it did not make a sound. "I don't know what it is," I said finally. "I've been told it's worth a lot of money."

"And someone's going to give you this money,"

she asked me, "in return for your stealing it?"

"Something like that," I said, remembering my promises.

"Then why did you drop into a tree?"

"Something was going wrong," I said.

"What was going wrong?"

"You'd know better than I would," I said. "You were watching me the whole time."

The coffeepot began to gurgle, and Ellington removed it from the fireplace and set it down, bubbling, on the table before fetching two cups and two saucers from a rack next to the sink. She poured two cups of coffee and let them steam in front of us for a moment on the table. The steam lingered in the air along with the odd, jumpy music. It was dark out the window, but I knew had it been daytime that we would have had a wide view of the Clusterous Forest. Ellington grabbed a pillow from the cot and knelt on the floor before replying.

"How did you know I was watching?" she asked quietly.

"I saw something glinting at me from the window of the cottage," I said, "right where those binoculars are sitting. You were watching me and my associate on the hawser. Why?"

"I've been watching this area for days," she said, and took a sip of her coffee. I left mine alone. It wasn't that I thought she had slipped laudanum into it. It was simply that I didn't like coffee. I didn't even like the way it smelled, dark and earthy like soil, but Ellington smiled a little as she sipped.

"What are you looking for?" I asked, and pointed to the Bombinating Beast. "This?"

She put down her coffee and smirked at the statue. The statue frowned back in reply. "I'm looking for something much more important than some silly statue," she said. "I'm looking for my father."

"What happened to him?"

She stood up. "Somebody took him—some terrible man. My father and I lived together in Killdeer Fields, a town farther up the road a ways."

"I've heard of it."

"It's a nice enough place," Ellington said, "although something was going on that was bothering my father, I could tell. And then one day I came home from school and he wasn't there. He wasn't there by dinnertime, and he wasn't there by bedtime, and in the morning a man called with a fearsome voice. He introduced himself as Hangfire and told me I'd never see my father again. That was six months ago. I've been looking the whole time, and I'm beginning to believe that what Hangfire told me was the truth." She walked to the cot and reached under it to show me an enormous, messy pile of notebooks, newspapers, envelopes, and parcels. "This is what I do," she said. "I've been following any lead I can find. I've interviewed dozens of people. I've checked on hundreds of rumors. I've written letters and telegrams, made phone calls, and knocked on doors. I've sent countless packages to people he knew, most of whom left Killdeer Fields after the flood. I send photographs of my father, copies of articles he's written, anything that might help people tell me where he is. A while ago I heard that Hangfire was hiding out here in Stain'd-by-the-Sea."

"He chose a good location. With so many abandoned buildings, this town is full of hiding places."

"Yes, I know. I've been living in this cottage ever since, hoping for a glimpse of him. If I find Hangfire, I know I'll find my father."

"But this Hangfire person wouldn't just give him back to you."

"No."

"So what will you do then?"

"Anything and everything," she told me, and it made me shiver a bit. She'd thought about her answer. She hadn't just said it, the way most people said most things.

"Why would Hangfire kidnap your father?" I asked her.

"That's the most mysterious part of all," Ellington said, and poured herself more coffee. "My father never hurt anyone. He's a kind, quiet man." Two tears rolled out of her eyes, and she brushed them away with her smooth black sleeve. "And he's a wonderful father. I've got to find him, Mr. Snicket. Will you help me?"

I had fallen out of one mystery and into another, and perhaps that was why I made another promise, this one as foolish and wrong as all the others. "I'll help you," I said. "I promise. But not tonight. Right now I have to leave. Thanks for the coffee."

"You didn't drink any."

"I told you I don't drink coffee," I said. "But come find me tomorrow and we can work together. I'm staying at the Lost Arms with my associate, S. Theodora Markson."

"What's the *S* stand for?" she asked, but then there was a knock at the door. The clock above the fireplace told me it was close to two in the morning. Ellington looked at me and asked the question that is printed on the cover of this book. It was the wrong question, both when she asked it and later, when I asked it myself. The right question in this case was "What was happening while I was answering the door?" but when the hinges stopped creaking, I was thinking only of the Officers Mitchum, who were standing there with matching stern eyes.

"Aren't you that Snicket lad?" Harvey Mitchum barked at me while Mimi Mitchum barked, "What are you doing here?"

I replied "yes" to the first question and "visiting a friend" to the second.

"What sort of young man visits friends in

the middle of the night?" asked the male officer suspiciously, sniffing the air and frowning.

"What sort of hanky-panky are you up to?" asked his wife.

I replied "a friendly one" and "I don't know what you're talking about," but I could tell these were the wrong answers.

"We need to talk to you, Snicket," Harvey Mitchum said. "There have been reports of a burglary. Somebody stole a very valuable statue in the shape of a mythical beast. Do you know anything about that?"

"I've always been interested in mythology," I said.

"That's not what I mean!" he snapped. "Your chaperone was hanging on the hawser and refused to tell us why."

"It's still too early to make assumptions," Mimi Mitchum said, "but it wouldn't be surprising if she's as big a criminal as you are, Snicket."

"I'd say she's a bigger criminal," her husband said.

"No, he is."

"She is."

"We can settle this later," Harvey Mitchum said with an annoyed look. "Right now we're going to search the premises for this valuable statue."

"Don't you need a warrant for that?" I asked.

"This isn't the Clusterous Forest," the female Officer Mitchum said, gesturing behind her back. "This is Stain'd-by-the-Sea, and we are the law here. Step aside, Snicket."

I stepped aside, but not before looking behind me and seeing with relief that the Bombinating Beast was not in plain sight on the table. Instead, Ellington Feint was in plain sight, holding her envelopes and parcels in an awkward pile in her arms.

"Good evening, Officers," she said.

"It's not *good evening*," Harvey Mitchum said sternly, "it's *bad behavior*. You should follow the example of my boy, Stewie. He knows better than to stay up late. That's why he's sleeping in the car right now."

"It keeps him calm," said Mimi.

"And alert," said Harvey.

"And good looking," added his mother.

"That's true," the male officer said. "Stew Mitchum is as cute as a button."

I tried to think of buttons I'd seen that liked to torture small animals, but I couldn't.

"Mr. Snicket," Ellington said quickly, "will you help me with these parcels?"

I took a step toward her. "Of course, Ms. Feint."

She smiled at the Mitchums. "Mr. Snicket and I were just about to take a walk to the mailbox to deliver these things."

"Wait until our search is over," Harvey

Mitchum said, "and we'll drive you there ourselves."

"Young people shouldn't be out at this hour," Mimi Mitchum said. "The Bombinating Beast might get you."

"That's a myth," I said.

"Ignore the bell and you'll find out," the male Mitchum said, and brushed past me to peer around the cottage. Ellington hefted a parcel into my hands that was about the size of a milk bottle. It was wrapped in newspaper, and I saw she'd hurriedly put a few stamps on it and scrawled an address:

S. THEODORA MARKSON
THE LOST ARMS
STAIN'D-BY-THE-SEA

The officers began rifling through Ellington's things, and she and I stood at the doorstep of the cottage. "Why didn't you address the package to me?" I whispered to her.

"I thought it would be suspicious if I were mailing a package to someone who was standing right next to me," she replied.

"Is the mail delivery reliable here?" I asked.

"Yes," she said. "You should have it by tomorrow morning. Surprisingly, delivery around here is very fast."

I tucked the wrapped statue under my arm. I had been told that if I found someone suitable during my apprenticeship, I could recommend them to our organization as a new member. It was too soon to make that decision, but it didn't feel too soon to smile at Ellington as the Mitchums muttered to themselves inside the cottage until they gave up.

"We give up," Harvey Mitchum said. "There's no statue in this cottage."

I took one step so I was standing outside.

"That's definitely true," I said. "Well, thanks for stopping by."

"Not so fast," Mimi Mitchum said. "We're driving you both to the mailbox and then home. I don't know what you ruffians are up to, but it's over for tonight. Get in the car and say hello to our adorable son."

Ellington and I followed the Officers Mitchum to their run-down station wagon and piled into the backseat, where Stew was waiting for us with a sleepy yawn and a cruel smile. "Lemony!" he said in the friendly voice he used to fool his parents. "It's so wonderful to see you again!"

I nodded at him, and he reached out his hand and gave me a hard pinch on the arm that the Officers Mitchum did not see. Ellington saw it, though, and reached forward herself and grabbed his wrist. Stew frowned, and I saw her fingernails digging into his skin. "It's lovely to meet you, Stew," she said. "I just know you and I are going to be lifelong friends."

Stew made a high-pitched sound certain boys find embarrassing, and we rode the rest of the way in silence. When we arrived in town, Mimi Mitchum brought the car to a squeaky halt and watched as Ellington and I dropped our packages into a lonely, scratched-up mailbox. The hinges of the mailbox door made a rough, unpleasant noise, and I was reluctant to drop my package in. So you're reluctant, I said to myself. Many, many people are reluctant. It's like having feet. It's nothing to brag about. The package made a muffled *clunk* as it landed, and then we got back into the station wagon and drove the short, empty distance to the Lost Arms. I thanked the officers for the ride and gave Ellington a secret smile and a wave and Stew nothing at all. The lobby of the Lost Arms was empty except for Prosper Lost, who was murmuring something into the telephone. I stopped for a moment by the plaster statue of the woman without arms or clothes and suddenly felt how tired I was.

"Yes," I said to her. "I suppose I'm in trouble," and I headed up the stairs to see.

CHAPTER EIGHT

Scolding must be very, very fun, otherwise children would be allowed to do it. It is not because children don't have what it takes to scold. You need only three things, really. You need time, to think up scolding things to say. You need effort, to put these scolding things in a good order, so that the scolding can be more and more insulting to the person being scolded. And you need chutzpah, which is a word for the sort of show-offy courage it takes to stand in front of someone and give them a good scolding, particularly if they are exhausted and sore and not in the mood to hear it.

S. Theodora Markson had all these things, plus a flowered nightcap over her wide, unrestrained hair, and when I opened the door of the Far East Suite, she gave me a scolding I'm sure I don't have to describe. You have doubtless been scolded about being more careful with valuable objects, or not wandering off by yourself, or causing someone to be worried sick about you, even if they appear to have taken time out from being worried sick to take a bath and change into a nightgown. Your valuable object may not have been a statue of the Bombinating Beast, and your wandering off may not have been dropping from a hawser into the trees below in the middle of a burglary, but otherwise Theodora's scolding of me was very much like all of the many scoldings all over the world. I stood in front of her and tried to make my face look like I was listening carefully and waited for the question that indicates a scolding is over.

"Don't you have anything to say for yourself?" she asked me.

"What happened when you arrived at the Sallis mansion?" I asked.

"Mrs. Sallis was not at home," she said, "and someone had told the Officers Mitchum that we were burglars. If I'd been foolish enough to have been holding the statue, I likely would have been arrested and put on the train to prison."

"I saw the red light from the Mitchums' car," I said. "That's why I dropped into the trees, so that we wouldn't be caught. After the police questioned you, they found me, but with some help I managed to hide the Bombinating Beast from them and drop it into the mailbox. We should receive it by morning."

Theodora blinked back at me. "You promise?"

I sighed. Every new promise was like something heavy I had to carry, with no place to put anything down. "Yes."

"You're still on probation," she said. "Get in bed. It's late."

I went into the bathroom to brush my teeth. It is good to brush your teeth when you are angry, because you brush harder and do a better job. I did not expect Theodora to understand what I had done, but I did expect her to be happier that I had gotten us out of trouble. But it didn't matter who was right and who was wrong, I told myself. You're still sharing a dreary hotel room with an unreliable chaperone, Snicket. Get some shut-eye. It's a word which here means sleep. The sheets had spiky wrinkles, and the pillow felt like a bag of marbles, and I had a very lonely feeling, thinking of how few people knew where I was or could come to me if I were in trouble. But I was too tired to be sad about it.

The next morning I learned why our room

was called the Far East Suite. It was located in the corner of the Lost Arms that was the farthest east, and so the very first rays of the sunlight came through the shutters and poked me in the eye. "Go play," I told the sunlight. "I'll catch up with you later." The sunlight insisted that I wake up right this very minute, so I sat up in bed and went into the bathroom to wash my face and change my clothes. Then I quietly let myself out of the Far East Suite and went down to the lobby, where Prosper Lost was standing behind the desk practicing his slippery smile. Rather than telling me that a package had arrived, he made me ask if a package had arrived, and then brought it out from underneath the desk. When I held it in my hands, my mood improved. I sat in the lobby for a few minutes to see if a woman with bad earrings would stop talking on the phone, but then gave up and decided to walk over to the library.

Dashiell Qwerty was chasing a couple of

moths out the front door. "Welcome," he said to me, his voice as deep as ever. "Can I help you?"

"Good morning," I said. "I don't think I need any help, thank you. I'm just looking for something to read."

"Be my guest," he said. "If you can't find something you like, I'll be unpacking a new shipment of zoological books in a little while."

"That reminds me," I said, as if I needed to be reminded. "Have you heard back from the Fourier Branch about that book I ordered?"

"*But I Cannot Meet You at the Fountain*, by that Belgian author?" he said. "No, nothing yet, I'm afraid. Although I did receive a somewhat mysterious request from that very branch. Someone is looking for a book I've never heard of before."

"What's it called?"

Qwerty reached into a pocket of his jangly leather jacket and pulled out a card. "The author is Don T. Worry," he read out loud, "and the title is *I'll Measure It Myself*. Sounds like a math textbook of some kind."

"Could be," I said. "Say, can I request another title?"

"Of course," he said. "From the Fourier Branch again?"

"Yes," I said.

Qwerty took a pencil from behind his ear while I reminded myself for a moment that his ragged hairstyle was probably very attractive to somebody. "And the author of the book you're looking for?"

"Please."

"Please?"

"Another Belgian," I said, "and the title is *Be Very, Very Careful*."

"Please, *Be Very, Very Careful*," the sublibrarian repeated. "Sounds like a scary story."

"I hope it isn't," I said, and excused myself

157

to find a book. I was in the mood for something I had read already, and for an hour I sat in my usual spot and read about someone who was a true friend and a good writer who lived on a bloodthirsty farm where nearly everyone was in danger of some sort. It was a good book, and I was sorry to put it back on the shelf. On my way out I found Qwerty leaning over an open cardboard box, fiddling with a stack of books.

"What are you doing?" I asked him.

"Checking the jackets," he said. "You'd be surprised at how often one book is slipped into the cover of another."

"Really?"

"Oh yes," the sub-librarian said with his usual blank look. "Very often you expect one thing from looking at the outside of it, but when you open it, there's something else entirely."

My stomach walked down a few stairs. "Thank you," I said, and quickly got out of the library and sat on the steps in the morning sun. I looked at Ellington Feint's handwriting on the label of the parcel, which had a faint scent I couldn't quite place. It was something from her cottage. I looked out at the tall metal sculpture in the middle of the lawn, its shape still unreadable to me. And then I tore open all the newspaper and held the object in my lap.

It was a bag of coffee, with a strong, earthy smell and a black cat stenciled on it. I looked at it for a long moment and even opened the bag to see if the Bombinating Beast was inside. Of course it wasn't. A car pulled up to the lawn, and I looked up to see Pip's smiling face behind the wheel of Bellerophon Taxi.

"Good morning, friend," he called to me. "I have a couple of extra doughnuts from Hungry's. Want one with your coffee?"

He was grinning at my bag, but I was in no mood to grin back. "Yes," I said. "And a ride?"

"Got a tip?"

"*The Long Secret* is a better book than the one

that comes before it," I said, opening the back door. "How's that?"

"That'll do," Pip said, "although Squeak and I have always preferred the one about the tap dancer and the lawyer."

"They're all good," Squeak squeaked from the floor of the car. "Where are you going? The lighthouse again?"

"That cottage near it," I said, "as quickly as you can."

"Handkerchief Heights?" Pip said, handing me a doughnut. "There's nobody there, friend."

"Let's hope you're wrong," I said, and the taxi hurried down the quiet street. I looked out the window and chewed and tried to think. I like a doughnut, particularly glazed. It had been some time since I had read the one about the tap dancer and the lawyer. Ellington Feint had hardly glanced at the statue when it was right there on her table. I smoothed out the newspapers that had been wrapped around the bag of coffee and saw they were old pages of *The Stain'd Lighthouse*. There was an advertisement for a play performed by the Stain'd Players at the Stain'd Playhouse some years earlier, starring an actress smiling in a faded photograph. The actress was playing the part of the heroine, Leslie Crosbie. Her name was Dame Sally Murphy. She didn't look happy to see me either.

By the time the taxi passed the Sallis mansion, I was wiping the sugar off my fingers, but that was about all I knew about what I was doing. I thanked the Bellerophon brothers and told them I hoped their father got better soon, and then I ran through the trees until I was standing at the door of the cottage. I knew at once that Ellington Feint was gone. Her suitcase was gone and her music was gone. But Pip and Squeak were wrong. There was somebody there. The door was open, and Moxie Mallahan was standing in the middle of the room.

"Lemony Snicket," she said to me, and stepped toward her typewriter. It lay ready on the table where I'd been offered coffee just the night before.

"What's the news, Moxie?" I asked.

"You tell me," Moxie said. "You're the one who called and told me to meet you here."

"I did no such thing."

"Snicket, stop fooling. I talked to you myself just a few minutes ago. You told me that you had the solution to the mystery of the Bombinating Beast, and to hurry down to Handkerchief Heights with my father."

"Is he here, too?"

"I couldn't wake him. What's going on?"

"That wasn't me on the phone," I said, and tried to think. My first thought was that Stew had phoned, pretending to be me, because he seemed just like that sort of person. No, Snicket, I thought to myself. Whoever called is interested in the Bombinating Beast. But the only people interested in it are Theodora and Mrs. Sallis—or, in other words, the woman who is going to help you steal it, and the woman who wants us to steal it in the first place. You're stuck. It makes no sense.

"Do you think someone was trying to lure us here?" Moxie asked, looking around the cottage.

"They were trying to lure you and your father out of your home," I said. "It's someone who's interested in that statue. They were hoping to steal it themselves while your house was empty."

"But my house isn't empty, Snicket."

"The trick didn't work," I said, "but it doesn't matter. The statue's not there anymore, but whoever called doesn't know that."

"Do you know who it is?"

I shook my head.

"Well, someone's been lurking around," Moxie said. "Handkerchief Heights is supposed to be locked up tight, but it looks like somebody's been living here. Somebody's been using the coffee-pot. Somebody's been drinking out of the cups. And somebody lit a fire with the wood that was piled up outside."

"And somebody's been eating your porridge," I muttered, looking quickly around the room.

"What?"

"Nothing. Was someone using an old-fashioned record player? Or a pair of binoculars? Or a suitcase full of clothing?"

"We never had anything like that here," Moxie said. "Why are you asking? What's going on? Who was here?"

"I don't know," I said, and it was true. I had talked to Ellington Feint, but I did not know what I knew about her. And you promised, Snicket, I told myself. You promised to help her. I stalked out of the cottage and found the ladder she'd used to get to the top of the tree, leaning against the side of Handkerchief Heights. I thought of the ladder I had hidden in the bathroom of the Hemlock Tearoom and Stationery Shop. If you hadn't put that ladder there, you wouldn't be here now, Snicket. You wouldn't be in this mess, or this mystery, or this messy mystery, or this mysterious mess. You'd be deep in a hole in the city with a measuring tape your friend gave you, doing something else you'd promised to do instead. I got mad and I kicked the ladder, and then I realized I was still holding the bag of coffee and threw it to the ground. It burst open. I picked up the torn paper of the bag so I wouldn't be littering, but there was nothing I could do about all the coffee in the grass. Maybe earthworms would want it. Theodora was probably drinking coffee right this minute, I thought to myself, waiting in the Far East Suite for me to bring her the statue I'd promised would be there in the morning. No wonder I was still on probation. I stared at the ripped, stenciled cat in my hands, and then out at the enormous, eerie view of the Clusterous Forest. I imagined it had been a pretty view of the sea back when the sea had been here. The water would have been very choppy, with small patches of foamy white darting this way and that. Like handkerchiefs, I thought, and the newspapers on the hawser, flapping in the breeze, would have looked like handkerchiefs, too. Washerwoman, she'd said. Laundry. Ellington Feint was a liar. I glared out at the rustling seaweed for quite some time.

Sometimes you have the time, the effort, and even the chutzpah to give someone a good scolding, but there's nobody around who deserves it.

Moxie came up behind me and put a hand on my shoulder. "So?" she asked.

"So?"

"What's going on, Snicket? Who do you think was living in the cottage? How do you think they broke in? When do you think they got there?" I didn't reply, but when I turned to face Moxie Mallahan, she didn't look interested in the answers to these questions. She wasn't even looking at me. Instead, her eyes were focused everywhere else, as if she were scanning for the answers at the lighthouse, or back in the cottage, or down a ways in the Sallis mansion, or off the edge of the cliff where I had first arrived in Stain'd-by-the-Sea. Then she asked a new question, and this question had my full attention. It is a question I had been asked three times before, and each time the answer was unpleasant. The answer is always unpleasant, because it is an unpleasant question.

"Where is that screaming coming from?" is what she asked.

CHAPTER NINE

There's an easy method for finding someone when you hear them scream. First get a clean sheet of paper and a sharp pencil. Then sketch out nine rows of fourteen squares each. Then throw the piece of paper away and find whoever is screaming so you can help them. It is no time to fiddle with paper. Even Moxie closed her typewriter up into its case with a brisk snap as we ran quickly through the trees.

There was no one in the trees or on the

brown grass. There was no one in trouble on the side of the cliff. It was as I feared. The screaming was coming from the Sallis mansion.

Moxie and I approached the mansion from the side, our feet crackling on birdseed dropped on the lawn. It was terrible to hear someone scream and be unable to help them. It went against all of my training. The confusing shapes of the building, with so many different styles of mansions jammed together, made it hard to tell exactly where the screams were coming from. One moment the desperate voice seemed to be coming from the tallest tower, but the next it seemed to be coming from the garden, with its fancy fountains and gray tent rippling in the breeze. The only things I knew for sure were that the screams were female and that I hoped they were Ellington's. I did not like to think about whether I was hoping she was in trouble or hoping I could rescue her.

Moxie was frowning at the mansion. "How

are we going to get inside?" she asked me. "Do you know how to pick a lock?"

"Not really," I said. "I received a grade of Incomplete. I know how to throw a rock through a window."

"Everyone knows how to throw a rock through a window," she said. "Come on. Let's go around to the front."

The screams didn't let up for a minute as we circled the building until we were standing at the driveway where Theodora and I had arrived just yesterday. "Hello?" I called, but there were only screams in reply. They were a bit louder now, and I could see why. The enormous front door was hanging wide open, like an arm bent very hard the very wrong way. That reminded me of another thing I had never been able to learn properly.

There was something I was always very good at, however, and that was teaching myself not to be frightened while frightening things are going on. It is difficult to do this, but I had learned. It is simply a matter of putting one's fear aside, like the vegetable on the plate you don't want to touch until all of your rice and chicken are gone, and getting frightened later, when one is out of danger. Sometimes I imagine I will be frightened for the rest of my life because of all of the fear I put aside during my time in Stain'd-by-the-Sea. I led Moxie inside the house. The screaming seemed to come from everyplace, echoing in the long, empty hallway. I thought I remembered a carpet on the floor when I had first entered the Sallis mansion, but I hadn't been paying much attention. The floor was bare now.

"The mansion is too big," I said. "We're going to have to split up."

"You want me to find whoever's screaming by myself?" Moxie asked.

"Get scared later," I told her, and hurried down the hallway and up a wide flight of stairs. There were rings on the floor under the banister, where potted plants had once been placed. Now they were gone. Everything seemed gone. There was a single lightbulb hanging from a wire in the ceiling above the staircase. Surely the Sallis family had enough money for a chandelier.

The screaming seemed louder at the top of the stairs, which led to another hallway with no carpets or furniture, simply rows of doors on either side. The first door revealed a room with nothing in it. So did the second. The third was a closet, and then a bathroom, and then three more rooms, but nowhere was there a person or even a scrap of furniture. The furnishings in the Sallis library, I remembered, had seemed wrong for the room. The room had been arranged hastily, using whatever furniture could be found, so Theodora and I would think the house was not deserted.

The door to the last room at the end of the hallway was difficult to open, because I had to take a moment to remind myself to be frightened later, perhaps when I was a grown man. It was a waste of time. The only thing in this room was a mattress, placed flat on the ground, with several blankets and pillows in a messy pile. I kicked through them. Nothing, Snicket. But why do you still hear the screaming? It took me a moment to notice that the screams were coming from a small grate in the ceiling, probably for heating the house. It was why the screams seemed to be everywhere, because every room in the house had such a grate. The grates all connected to the heater. There was another sound, too, through the grate. At first it sounded like the rustling of the Clusterous Forest. Most people keep their heaters in the basement.

I ran downstairs, through a living room empty of everything except an enormous, smooth window overlooking the strange view, and across a kitchen with no refrigerator, no stove, and no pots or pans hanging from a bare rack. Moxie had figured out the same thing I had, and was

pushing hard against a small white door. I hurried to help her. The door struggled to open, as if someone were on the other side, pushing back, but Moxie and I managed. There was no one on the other side, just a large rock, about the size of a good dictionary, that someone had wedged up against the door that led to the basement steps. We stood on the top step and looked down at something that would frighten us later.

The Sallis basement was enormous, about the size of a huge swimming pool or even a small lake, and right then, also like a huge swimming pool or a small lake, it was a body of water. The room was about half full of brown, churning water, slapping against the walls of the basement and slowly climbing the steps toward us as the water continued to rise. For a moment it appeared that the head of Mrs. Murphy Sallis was floating in the middle of the basement, blindfolded and screaming. But then I realized she must have been tied to something, with the water rising above her and just inches away from reaching her mouth. She was about to drown. Moxie put her typewriter next to the door and started to walk down the stairs.

"No," I said loudly over the rushing of the water, and grabbed her shoulder.

"We have to help her," Moxie said, her brow furrowing under her hat.

"Not like that," I said, trying to think quickly. On the far wall of the basement, I could see the top edge of a window, otherwise covered in water. I leaned down to pick up one end of the large stone. "Help me," I said. "Everyone knows how to throw a rock through a window."

We picked up the rock and heaved it at the window. It is more fun to throw rocks when you don't have to care about where they will land, but the window was large enough and the rock was large enough that it wasn't too hard to hit one with the other. The window broke with a muted shatter, and water immediately began to rush out of the basement, as if we'd pulled the plug. Mrs. Sallis kept screaming, even when the water was low enough that we could walk down the stairs and untie her. The knots were difficult, but Moxie was good with them—better than I was, if I want to write the truth.

I left Moxie to her rope work and walked over to the source of the water, which was still gushing from a far corner. It was gushing from a large vat, wide enough for a grown-up to fit into, not that anybody would want to. It was fashioned out of gray bricks, with a large rusty lever alongside it. The lever moved easily, and the water stopped immediately. An underground spring, I realized, must have run under the Sallis mansion. It was a basement well, worked by a simple but clever pump. Well, well, well, I thought. No wonder the science reporters did research here.

Mrs. Sallis was tied to a chair, one of the chairs I had seen in the library, with large, puffy cushions that were now ruined. But Mrs. Sallis wasn't ruined. As soon as Moxie got her hands free, she reached up and tore off the blindfold, which I thought would calm Mrs. Sallis down. Instead she went ape, an expression I've always liked, although there was no ape who was ever as loud as she was.

"*Where is he?*" she cried.

"Who?" Moxie said.

"There's nobody here," I said, but this was the wrong thing to say. Her eyes widened further, and she looked so frightened that when she had looked frightened before, it no longer counted as looking frightened.

"*Get out of here!*" she screamed. "*Leave this house at once!*"

"I was hoping for 'Thank you for rescuing me' instead, Mrs. Sallis," I said.

Moxie gave me a curious look. "That's not Mrs. Sallis," she said.

There was still plenty of water in the basement, and I felt it soaking me from the knees on down. If someone wanted to torture me until I told them a critical piece of information, all they would have to do is get my socks wet. It feels terrible. The water was too dirty for me to tell if the old woman was wearing socks as she limped up from her chair and drew herself up to her full height and looked at us imperiously. "Imperiously" is a word you may not know, but you've seen it on the faces of people who believe themselves to be much, much better than you are.

"I am Mrs. Murphy Sallis," she said, "and I command you to get out of my home."

"You're not Mrs. Murphy Sallis," Moxie insisted, and then turned to me. "In fact, there is no Mrs. Murphy Sallis. I've known Mrs. Sallis my entire life, and her first name is Dot."

"This is Dame Sally Murphy," I said, "Stain'd-by-the-Sea's most famous actress. She's a local legend."

The old woman's expression changed, like

water was also rushing out of her face. She sat back down in the chair with a squishy thud and nodded sullenly at us. "It's always nice to meet a fan of the theater," she said.

"I thought she looked familiar," Moxie said. "*The Stain'd Lighthouse* put her picture on the front page a dozen times. But how did you know her, Snicket? What is going on? Why did she say she was Mrs. Sallis? When did you know she was an impostor?"

"Let's let her answer," I said.

"*I don't have to tell you!*" the old woman shrieked. It was probably the sort of performance that people loved at the Stain'd Playhouse. "*Leave me alone! Have respect for your elders!*"

Respecting one's elders is difficult enough, but when they are soaked with water and have proved themselves to be dishonest, it is nearly impossible. I leaned down to look her in the eye. "Where is Ellington?" I said. "Where is the Bombinating Beast?"

"*Leave at once!*" she shrieked, but she no longer looked imperious. She looked frightened. She had not learned to save it for later, or perhaps she had, and very frightening things had happened before I'd gotten here. Perhaps they'd even happened before I arrived in town.

"Why did you tell me the statue was yours?" I asked her. "Who put you in this basement?"

"*He* did," she replied. "Now get out! I have my family to think of!"

I put a hand on her damp shoulder. "I think I can help you," I said, "but you must tell me what's going on."

"You can't help me," the old woman snarled, and shook off my hand. "*He's* the only one who can help me. You're just a child."

I was tempted to take off my wet socks, and not only because they were uncomfortable. "I'm part of an organization," I said, "that I'm sure can be of service."

Sally Murphy's eyes widened, and I could tell

she was even more frightened than she had been. "*Get out!*" she screamed, and like many actresses she practiced this line over and over again. "*Get out! Get out! Get out!*"

"I meant to tell you," I said. "My deafness was cured by a treatment of root beer, so you don't have to shout at me."

"*Get out!*" she continued to shout, and I got out. I turned away from the old woman and stalked up the stairs, almost tripping on Moxie, who was sitting on one step, furiously pounding away at her typewriter.

"So?" she asked.

"So?"

"What organization were you talking about, exactly?" she asked me, her eyes excited and careful.

"I can't tell you," I said, moving past her.

She snapped her typewriter closed and hurried after me up the steps and through the vacant kitchen. "Why not?" she said to me.

I continued through the mansion, my footsteps echoing in the empty rooms. The Sallis
mansion had been empty for a long time, so
nobody noticed when someone had snuck in.
They'd used a few scraps of furniture and a few
dull books to make a fake library, and hired Sally
Murphy to make a fake Mrs. Sallis, and then
hired Theodora and myself, who wouldn't know
the house was supposed to be empty or recog-
nize Stain'd-by-the-Sea's local legend. The plan
was to get us to steal the Bombinating Beast and
then have us caught by the Officers Mitchum.
With us in jail and Sally Murphy drowned in
the basement, the villain would have everything he
wanted, including the statue. But I had mucked
up the plan by dropping off the hawser. And then
Ellington Feint had stolen the statue for her
own mysterious reasons, and now she was in the
middle of this treachery, too. It was just a small
wooden object—*that old thing*, Moxie had called
it—but it was causing danger wherever it went,

the way an octopus is generally harmless but can stain everyone with ink in an instant.

By now I was at the front door, and Moxie was still asking me questions. "Where are you going? Why won't you talk to me? What's going on?"

I stopped on the driveway, outside the mansion. "I don't know what's going on," I said, "but it's dangerous. We just had to rescue a woman from drowning."

"She didn't seem like she wanted to be rescued," Moxie replied. "She said only *he* could help her, even though *he* put her in the basement to begin with. Who is *he*?"

"Someone who sounded like me," I said.

"What?"

"I think," I said, thinking out loud, "that his name is Hangfire."

"What?" Moxie said again, and then "Who? Why? How? Tell me the story, Snicket."

I thought about Theodora, who was probably

angry at me all over again. It was afternoon, and the statue had not arrived, as I had promised it would. I had to stop making promises. "I don't know the story," I told Moxie. "This whole town is a mystery. It's something we can't see, remember?"

"I'm a journalist," Moxie said. "I can help you solve it."

"Then go back to the cottage," I said, "and look for clues. There was someone living there, a girl a little older than us. I've got to find her."

"A girl?" she repeated with a frown. "What does she have to do with this?"

"I don't know," I said, and started to walk down the driveway.

"Come home with me," Moxie said. "You can dry off, and we can compare notes."

"I've got to get into town," I said.

Moxie frowned again and put her hands on her hips. "Lemony Snicket, you can shoo me off to Handkerchief Heights. But I know more about this town than you do. You can't solve this mystery alone."

"I know I can't," I admitted, but I started walking alone toward the road.

CHAPTER TEN

By the time I reached the streets of Stain'd-by-the-Sea, the town still quiet and unpeopled and my socks still wet and squishy, I had figured out what to look for. At first it seemed like there was too much to find. I had to find whoever had broken into the Sallis mansion. I had to find whoever had tried to drown Dame Sally Murphy. I had to find Ellington Feint, and her father, and whoever had captured him. And I had to find out why all this had happened. But halfway down a gray and empty block, I realized all these beads were strung together. Everyone was after the Bombinating Beast, and if I got my hands on that black, spooky statue, then everything else would try to find me instead. The deserted blocks of Stain'd-by-the-Sea seemed like an easier place to find one mysterious item than a bustling city full of them. I thought of all the mysterious items back in the city, and how difficult it would be for someone I knew to get her hands on one in particular, particularly without my help.

I wanted to see her. Communicating through made-up book titles was not enough. I could almost hear her saying to me, "Well, L, where was the last place you saw this statue?"

"On the table," I imagined saying, "in Handkerchief Heights, right before the Officers Mitchum knocked on the door."

"And what was happening while you were answering the door?" She always had a knack for knowing the right question to ask.

"Ellington was wrapping the statue in newspaper. Then she did the same for a bag of coffee. She gave me the coffee with Theodora's address on it and carried the other package with all the other things she was mailing."

"And did she drop it in the mailbox?"

"Yes."

"Are you sure?"

"Yes, I saw her."

"And did you see the address she wrote on the newspaper?"

"No," I said, "but she must have been mailing it to herself."

"She could have been mailing it to an accomplice."

"She was living in that cottage all by herself," I said. "Besides, if Ellington had an accomplice, she never would have asked me to help her."

"Well, she didn't mail it to Handkerchief Heights, or the package would have been there in the morning. You or Moxie would have found it. Think, L."

"You know I hate it when you call me L."

"Where did she mail it?"

I took a long sip of root beer and thought. As long as I was having an imaginary conversation, I saw no reason why I couldn't have an imaginary root beer to help me think. "To the one reason she ventures into town," I said finally.

"And where is that?"

"Black Cat Coffee. Corner of Caravan and Parfait."

"Good work, L. You're doing all right by yourself."

"Are you?"

She didn't answer, of course, and she didn't talk to me the rest of the way. I still didn't know my way around all the streets of Stain'd-by-the-Sea, so my steps were unsure. Normally one could ask directions of passersby, but without a soul on the streets, there was nobody to ask;

and normally one can find a map at a hotel, but I didn't want to go to the Lost Arms. Theodora was likely there, devoting her time, effort, and chutzpah to a much better scolding than the one I had been given the previous night. So I found my own way. I headed toward the tall pen-shaped building and eventually came across Caravan, a wide street, empty as all the others, that wandered its way around town like it didn't know where it was going either. Finally I hit Parfait, a narrow lane with a cold wind, and there was Black Cat Coffee, the sole business on a block that was otherwise boarded up. The only sign of life was a large wooden sign that didn't even have the name of the place, just the large, stenciled cat I recognized from the bag of coffee.

When I pushed open the doors and walked in, my first thought was that there was finally somewhere in Stain'd-by-the-Sea that was bustling with life. My second thought was that there was nobody there. Black Cat Coffee was a long, narrow room with an enormous counter in the center, but not one person was sitting on one of the stools. Behind the counter was a mass of shiny machinery of a sort I had not seen, with tubes and levers and spouts and panels all loud and busy with activity, but there was nobody there making it go. And in the corner was a piano playing music, but when I stepped closer, I saw it was a player piano, which can play all by itself. It sounded like it might have been the same music Ellington had been playing in the cottage, but perhaps that was just because I was thinking about her. I had forgotten to ask her the name of the tune. Well, there was no one to ask here, not anything. There was no one to ask if there was a package waiting for Ellington Feint. There was no one to ask if Ellington Feint had been there already to collect the package. And there was no one to ask to see a menu.

"Hello?" I asked, which is what everyone asks when they enter a room they are surprised to find empty. I stepped closer to the counter and saw three large brass buttons, right in a row, that had been built into a place on the counter where there were no seats. The buttons were each labeled with a brass letter: *A*, *B*, and *C*.

When I pressed *C*, the machinery behind the counter whirred to life. Steam clouded out from a row of holes toward the top of the machinery, and an enormous round bulb, like a lightbulb but made of metal, began to quake noisily. A small door opened, and a funnel came out on a long metal spring, and soon something was pouring from the bulb through the funnel into something that looked like a radio. Finally, a metal claw emerged from someplace with a small white saucer holding a small white cup, which got filled to the brim with something that smelled dark and familiar. The claw deposited the cup and saucer right in front of the *C* button, where it sat steaming at me.

"Coffee?" I said out loud, and then, because I

had offered it to myself, felt it would be polite to tell myself "No, thank you."

When I pressed *B*, different parts of the machine began to tremble, and a different kind of steam began to cloud from a different row of holes. Two devices that looked like metal hands began to wrestle over something white and sticky, which was then pounded by a pair of loud wooden hammers. Finally the whole mess was pushed into a door, and a clock began ticking, and after some time a bell rang and the door opened and something slid down a slide to stop in front of the *B* button. A better smell filled the empty room.

"And *B* is for bread," I said, and it was delicious.

When I pressed the *A* button, the machinery stayed quiet, and for a second I thought it was an aberration. But then right above me was a mighty scraping, as if the entire building were being lifted by a crane, and I stepped aside as a huge part of the ceiling lowered at a strict, sharp angle, revealing a staircase that led up and away from where I was standing.

"Attic," I said. It was a good place to keep packages. The music from the piano told me there was nothing to worry about, but I climbed the staircase with my belly full of bread and butterflies. I was tired of surprises in strange rooms. But the attic of Black Cat Coffee was just another big room with nobody in it. Along the wall were a few cupboards, and shelves with bags of coffee on them. There was a long table with envelopes and packages stacked in separate piles, as if quite a few people collected their mail at Black Cat Coffee instead of at home. I wondered why. There were not that many packages. There was a small box marked MEDICAL SUPPLIES addressed to a Dr. Flammarion. There was a long tube marked ELECTRICAL EQUIPMENT addressed to nothing more than a pair of initials that were unfamiliar. And then there was a package about the size of a bottle of milk, wrapped in newspaper with a handwriting I recognized immediately.

I unwrapped it carefully. It was the Bombinating Beast. It did not look happy to be found, but I was happy to see it. Everything in the world, I thought to myself. Every single thing, Snicket, has a place, and this statue is now with you.

The sun was dying when I stepped back out into the street, and the statue felt like it was bombinating under my arm. It was not actually buzzing, of course, but it made me nervous to carry something that everyone wanted, even though I'd rewrapped it carefully. I thought of the Far East Suite and how few hiding places it had, and took a detour, walking quickly past the Lost Arms and toward a place that had so many secrets already that one more wouldn't hurt.

"Welcome," Dashiell Qwerty said as I entered the library. "I see you're still carrying the same burden I saw you with this morning."

"So it would appear," I said.

"Are you checking on your loan requests from the Fourier Branch?" he asked, his face as blank as usual. "Because I haven't heard anything back just yet."

"I was just looking for something to read," I said.

Now Qwerty smiled and made a wide gesture with his hand and the sleeve of his leather jacket. "Make yourself at home," he said, and I did. I had been in Stain'd-by-the-Sea for only a couple of days, and already I had spent more time here than I had in the meager room I was sharing with Theodora. Even though he had curious hair and a blank expression, I felt more comfortable with my sub-librarian than I did with my chaperone. And the rows of shelves, though as unpeopled as the streets I'd just walked, made me feel better than just about anything in Stain'd-by-the-Sea. I was at home, which is why

I decided it was acceptable to hide something in the shelves, just for a little while. I searched for a long book that looked boring, and settled on something called *An Analysis of Brown, Black, and Beige*, hoping that nobody would be interested in the study of ordinary colors for at least a day. I unwrapped the statue, pulled the book from the shelf, and pushed the Bombinating Beast into the empty space as far as it could go, before replacing the book.

Now, I realized, I needed something to wrap the newspapers around. Qwerty had noticed my package, and he would notice if I didn't have it when I left. One large book, or perhaps three medium-sized ones, would be a good substitute, and I knew at once which three books I would pick. It made me feel a bit guilty to sneak books out of the library, but I promised myself I'd return them promptly. I found the titles at once and sat down at my usual table. I was in no hurry to return to my hotel. I could take some time to read. Even with everything that had happened, there was something else that had been on my mind since morning.

I ended up reading until Qwerty told me it was closing time, when I thanked him and strolled down the proper aisle, pretending to return the books. Instead, I slipped them into the newspaper and gave him a wave good-bye as I stepped outside. It was quite late. I was not sure *The Long Secret* was the best. All three of the books were good. I walked across the scraggly lawn, hoping I would find Ellington Feint. Perhaps she would read them, too, and we could have a good-natured argument over which was best. Nothing firms up a friendship like a good-natured argument. But you're not friends, I told myself, with Ellington Feint.

My thoughts went like this all the way back to the Lost Arms, where a dented, familiar taxi was parked outside. Through the window I could see Pip sound asleep against the steering wheel. I envied him as I walked into the lobby. Theodora was standing at such an angle that the head of the plaster statue looked like it was peeking out of her hair, but she was in no mood for me to point that out.

"Where have you been?" she said in a terrible voice. "I have been worried sick, Snicket."

"I'm sorry about that," I said.

"I just received an upsetting phone call," she told me, and began to pace up and down in front of the plaster woman. "This is already after the police suspect you of burglary and the vandalism of a streetlamp. And now you were playing with a little girl near a well. You're supposed to be my apprentice, Snicket, not my stomachache!"

I was tired of all these mysterious phone calls, particularly when I had been unable to use the phone myself. "Who called you?" I asked.

"Mr. Mallahan," Theodora said. "He was very upset and told me to tell you that you're not allowed near his daughter anymore."

"I don't think that was Mr. Mallahan."

"Don't be daft, Snicket. He said he was Mr. Mallahan, and he sounded just like him."

"There's much more to this mystery than we know," I said. "That's why it isn't safe to have the Bombinating Beast here."

"You mean that isn't it?" Theodora said, pointing to the parcel under my arm. "You mean you don't even have what you were assigned to retrieve in the first place? I told you before that people are watching us. If you fail me in this task, my reputation will suffer."

"You're already ranked last," I said, and regretted it at once. I had not been raised by people who raised their hands to me, so I had not yet learned that with some people if you say the wrong thing at the wrong time, you will be hit.

Theodora's eyes widened with shock at what I had said to her. "Not sensible!" she shouted.

"Not proper!" And with a growl that sounded like something I would have expected from a legendary beast, she raised her gloved palm up in the air. She likely wanted to slap me, but I do not know if she would have. What I do know is that we were interrupted by the voice of Prosper Lost, who was standing in the booth in the corner of the lobby, calling to me.

"Lemony Snicket," he said, "you have a phone call."

Theodora uttered a high-pitched shriek of annoyance, turned on her heels, and stalked up the stairs. I watched her go and nodded at Prosper Lost, who had dropped the phone, letting it dangle from its cord, to walk back to his post at the desk. I walked toward the phone booth, the newspaper crinkling underneath my arm. I wondered who was calling me, and I wondered it out loud. I asked the question printed on the cover of this book, and once again it was the wrong one to ask. The right question was "When had I heard this person's voice before?" but that question didn't occur to me, not even when I picked up the receiver and heard the terrible things that were said.

CHAPTER ELEVEN

"Hello?"

"It's Ellington," said the voice out of the phone. Her voice sounded breathy and worried, or perhaps that was just the phone. "I'm in trouble."

"Where are you?" I asked.

"He's captured me," the voice said. "I need your help."

"Hangfire?"

"Hangfire." I am not a hairy person, but each one of my hairs stood up and showed off at the sound of his name. The sound seemed to have a similar effect on Prosper Lost, who stepped back out from behind his desk and took a sudden interest in dusting off the cushions of the sofa. I wish my Beginning Eavesdropping instructor had been there in the lobby to flunk him.

"He found me in the cottage and dragged me away and threw me into this room. I'm frightened."

"Thank goodness you found a telephone," I said.

"Do you have the statue?"

"The Bombinating Beast?" I said, just so I could see Prosper Lost take an interest in an even closer cushion. Dust, dust, dust, Mr. Lost, I thought.

"Do you have it, Lemony?"

I liked it better when Ellington called me Mr. Snicket. Of course, I liked it better when I was actually talking to Ellington. "I don't think it's wise to answer that question on the phone."

"Of course," the voice replied. "Well, if you have it, bring it to Thirteen Hundred Blotted Boulevard."

"If I have it," I said, "I should bring it to a certain address in the middle of the night, instead of keeping it here, where it might be safe?"

"If he gets the statue, I won't be his prisoner anymore. Please hurry, Lemony."

"It was certainly nice of him to let you pack your things before he dragged you away," I said. "Even your record player was gone. What was the name of that tune, again?"

"Hurry," said the voice again, and the line went dead. I had to admit it did really sound like Ellington Feint, just as it must have sounded like Mr. Mallahan, and it must have sounded like me when Moxie picked up the phone. I looked at the parcel in my hands.

"Is there anything I can assist you with?" Prosper Lost said, and clasped his dusty hands together. I thought suddenly of another word for obsequious that was much more insulting.

"Yes," I said, and handed him the books wrapped in newspaper. "Can you please hold this package for me?"

"Oh yes," he said, kowtowing.

"Thank you," I said. "I think someone might ask for it very soon."

"At this hour?" he asked.

"You'd be surprised what might happen at this hour," I said, and walked out of the hotel to knock on the side of Bellerophon Taxi. Pip opened his eyes and rolled down the window.

"Egad, Snicket, don't you ever sleep?" he asked.

"Doesn't your father ever drive this heap?" I replied.

"He's sick, like I told you," Pip said. "You need a ride?"

"You need a tip?"

"Sure."

"I think you might be right about the tap dancer book."

"That's not a tip."

"Sorry," I said. "It's late. Can I owe you one?"

Pip looked down and nudged his brother. "Wake up, Squeak. We have a fare."

"Where are we going?" Squeak asked from the brake pedals.

"Thirteen Hundred Blotted Boulevard," I said.

"There's nothing there, Snicket," Pip said. "Out of all the empty neighborhoods in Stain'd-by-the-Sea, that's got to be the emptiest."

"There's not a single building left on Blotted Boulevard," Squeak agreed as I climbed into the backseat.

"You know when someone tells you there's a monster under the bed?" I asked them. "And you know, of course, that there's no such thing, but you just have to check under the bed anyway? Well, that's what we're doing here."

"Sounds like a wild ride to me," Pip said, starting the engine.

"Speaking of wild rides, if you haven't read *The Wind in the Willows*, you really should," I told them.

"Now *that's* a tip," Pip said. "Let's get a move on."

We got a move on. With a roaring engine and squeaky brakes, the Bellerophon brothers took us quickly out of the less faded neighborhoods of Stain'd-by-the-Sea, and we were soon on streets without a single business on them. Then we were on streets without a single light on them—even the automated stoplights had vanished from the corners. And then we were on Blotted Boulevard, and as Squeak had said, there was not a single building as far as the eye could see. The taxi paused on the very first block of the Boulevard, and on either side of the wide street were flat, empty lots, stretching out for thirteen blocks with only the occasional small pile of rubble asking for attention.

Ellington Feint was not being held captive at 1300 Blotted Boulevard, but I had Pip and Squeak take us all the way down the street anyway, until we stopped at a particularly flat, particularly empty lot. I thought of some of the secret passageways underneath certain buildings back in the city, but I could see at once there wasn't a door or anything else that could lead to a secret. There was simply nothing.

"What did I tell you?" squeaked Squeak.

"You were right," I said. "Sorry to waste your time. Let's head back."

"You're not wasting our time, Snicket," Pip said with a tired grin. "You and your chaperone are the most interesting thing to happen in this town in quite some time."

I grinned back, and judging by the sound of the brakes, I guessed Squeak was smiling, too. "Good night," I said when we were back at the Lost Arms. Prosper Lost was standing on the sagging porch of the hotel, watching us pull up.

"Good evening," he said in his thin voice. "Welcome back."

"Thank you," I replied. "Did anyone come for the package?"

"A gentleman came as soon as you left," he said. "He took the package but seemed most displeased, so I sent him up to the Far East Suite."

"You did *what*?" I asked.

"Sent him up to your room, so he might have a word with Ms. Markson," Prosper Lost said, with the tiniest of smiles.

I hurried past him through the lobby. The owner of the Lost Arms followed me, without even pretending to be interested in dusting something. When we reached the stairs, I could hear somebody scream.

"Should I call the police?" Prosper asked me.

"No," I said. "Find a clean sheet of paper and a sharp pencil, and sketch out nine rows of fourteen squares each," and I left him gaping at me and ran up the stairs. The door to the

Far East Suite was wide open, with a stain on the doorknob that looked green and sticky. Get scared later, I told myself.

S. Theodora Markson could have been an opera singer. Her screams were quite loud even through the handkerchief that had been tied around her mouth. The handkerchief matched the white strips of cloth that were tied around her arms and her legs as she wriggled this way and that on the bed, like a butterfly whose cocoon turns out to be more difficult than planned. The rest of the place was ransacked, a word for something that is fun to do to someone else's room but no fun to have done to yours. Every scrap of Theodora's clothing had been flung out of the chest of drawers, and my suitcase had been dragged out from under the cot and emptied all over the floor. It is embarrassing to see someone's clothing tossed everyplace, although it is hard to say why. The table had been tipped over and the shutters torn down from the open window. I checked the bathroom, but no one was there. Hangfire had left through the window. The only thing that hadn't been wrecked in the room was the painting of a little girl holding a dog with a bandaged paw. She looked like she wanted to remind me to untie Theodora. I tried to untie the handkerchief first, but the knot was complicated. Theodora wagged her head and blinked her eyes in the direction of the bathroom and indicated that I might find a knife there. I looked but found no knife. Theodora indicated that I should look again. There wasn't a knife when I looked again. Finally, with much more complicated head motions and faster blinking, she made clear that she didn't mean a knife but some nail clippers. I found them and, with much effort, cut through the handkerchief over her mouth so she could yell at me freely.

"This is *your* fault, Snicket!"

When someone is tied up, it is almost always the fault of whoever did the tying. Also, when someone is tied up, they are likely to be very upset and to say things they might not mean. "What did he look like?" I said, starting on the cloth that bound her arms. It was a ripped sheet, I realized, but the edges were too jagged to have been cut, and there was moisture here and there on the jagged edges. He had used his teeth. I did not like to think about a person ripping a sheet into strips with their teeth. It seemed too fierce or too wild a thing to do.

"He was wearing a mask," Theodora said. "He said he was going to kill me." Her eyes kept blinking. She was crying. Crying is like the opposite of scolding, because adults are hardly ever allowed to do it. "He's going to kill us both, Snicket, if he doesn't get his hands on that statue. He's a terrible man. He's despicable. He's loathsome, a word which here means terrible and despicable. We have to give the Bombinating Beast to him."

"That's not what we promised," I reminded

her as a strip of sheet slipped away from her wrists. "We promised to return the Bombinating Beast to its rightful owner."

Theodora took a deep breath and the nail clippers from me to free her feet. "Then why don't we just give the statue to Mrs. Sallis?"

"That wasn't Mrs. Sallis," I said. "That was an actress. This whole assignment has been a scheme, and Hangfire has been behind it. He imitates voices on the phone. He threatens people. He's doing everything he can to get his hands on that statue. We can't give it to him."

"You are just an apprentice on probation," Theodora said sternly. "You will do whatever your chaperone says. Now get out of here. I can hardly stand to look at you."

"But, Theodora—"

"*Get out!*" she cried, and buried her head in the ransacked bed. Her shoulders began to shake beneath her hair. I wiped the doorknob clean with my handkerchief and shut the door quietly behind me and left the Far East Suite very tired. This was the second person I had rescued today from Hangfire's treachery, and neither of them had been grateful. Although I did not drink coffee, I understood what Ellington had said about needing something restorative, and walked out of the Lost Arms, passing Prosper Lost, who was bent over a piece of paper, counting on his fingers. I tossed my ruined handkerchief in the garbage. It smelled salty and wretched. Outside, Pip and Squeak were asleep again in the taxi, and I did not have the heart to wake them. I walked. Caravan and Parfait was closer than I thought. As before, there appeared to be no one in the place, although the piano was playing that interesting and complicated tune, and the shiny machinery was ready to make me either B or C. But I was looking instead at A, and at the metal staircase that led up out of the only reason a friend of mine ventured into town.

Had I been paying attention, I would have noticed that most of the mail was now gone from the big room at the top of the stairs. I should have paid attention. But instead I just looked at the person with her back to me. Next to her were a large, striped suitcase and an oddly shaped case perfect for holding an old-fashioned record player. Hanging from her shoulder was a green purse shaped like a long, zippered tube as she stood and looked at the shelves filled with stenciled bags of coffee. Then she turned around, and I paid attention to her dark, dark hair, and her eyebrows, each one coiled over like a question mark, and her green eyes underneath.

"Lemony Snicket," she said.

"Ellington Feint," I said, and it was only then that I saw that smile of hers, the one that could have meant anything.

221

CHAPTER TWELVE

"Shall we get some coffee?" Ellington asked me.

"That's the wrong question," I said.

"Oh yes," she said. "You don't drink it. Well, there's no root beer here, or tea or milk. I don't even think Black Cat Coffee has water."

"That's not what I mean," I said.

"I know what you mean," Ellington said, and strode past me. Her feet *clang, clang, clang*ed as she began to walk down the metal stairs. "You mean, 'How could you have stolen that statue from me, Ellington?' Well, if it makes you feel any better, somebody stole it from me. It was supposed to be right here in this attic, but now it's gone, and I'm lost if I don't get it back."

"I have it," I said.

The girl stopped. Ellington pointed one of her long, black nails at me. "You have the Bombinating Beast?"

"Yes," I said.

"Mr. Snicket, please give it to me," she said, *clang*ing back up to look me in the eye. "It's very valuable. I need it. I need to have it by morning."

"It's not valuable, Ms. Feint," I said. "It's just a piece of junk."

"It's valuable to me," Ellington said, and I could see it was true. *Anything and everything*, she'd said.

"Why?" I asked. "What is it for? What does it do?"

"I don't know."

"Then how can it be valuable to you?"

Ellington looked around the room as if someone might be hiding among the envelopes and coffee beans. "Because it's valuable to Hangfire," she said finally. "If I give it to him, he will free my father."

"I thought so," I said.

"I thought you thought so," she said.

"I'd like to help you rescue your father," I said, "but I promised to give the Bombinating Beast back to its rightful owner."

"You also promised to help me," she reminded me. "If you don't give it to me, I may never see my father again."

"You can't trust this man Hangfire," I said. "The last person who helped him in his schemes was almost drowned."

"Mrs. Sallis?"

"It wasn't Mrs. Sallis," I said, "but it doesn't matter. Hangfire is a villain, Ms. Feint. He's a terrible man. You can't associate with him."

"I don't care about Hangfire," Ellington said. "I care about my father." She sighed and put down the long, zippered tube. "Hangfire's kidnapped a number of people in order to get them to participate in his schemes. My father is one of them. I've been following them for a long time, but I was always too far behind. Then, just a few days ago, my father called me and told me to come to Stain'd-by-the-Sea. Hangfire was holding him there, he told me, but he would be set free in exchange for the Bombinating Beast."

"That's funny," I said, "because you just called me a little while ago and told me to come to Thirteen Hundred Blotted Boulevard. You were being held there, but Hangfire would set you free in exchange for the same thing."

Ellington blinked at me in confusion. "I did no such thing."

"I know you didn't," I said. "Hangfire has the ability to mimic people's voices. That's how he manages to perform his treachery while still staying in the background. He wore a mask when he attacked Theodora. Probably very few people know what he even looks like."

"Then how can we find him?"

"Well, he must be close by," I said, and Ellington looked nervously down the stairs. "He'd have to be someplace where he could keep an eye on Mrs. Sallis—and on you."

"Then I've got to give him the statue," Ellington said, her green eyes fierce and worried. "Hangfire told me that I must have it by morning. Every part of my plan went perfectly. Once I learned that the statue belonged to the Mallahans, I moved into Handkerchief Heights and waited for days for an opportunity to break into the lighthouse and take it. Then one night I saw you and your wild-haired associate go into the lighthouse and leave through the hawser. You even had the luck to drop right into my tree. When you showed me the Bombinating Beast, I knew the time had come."

"You would have gotten away with it," I said, "except you told me all about Black Cat Coffee. Why?"

Ellington shrugged, and her cheeks got a little red. "Because I like you, Mr. Snicket," she said. "I thought you might find this place interesting, even if you don't drink coffee."

"I do find it interesting," I said. "I find this whole story interesting. I promised to help you, Ms. Feint, and I will. Your father has fallen into wicked hands, but it is not necessary to be wicked ourselves. We can rescue him without kowtowing to a villain like Hangfire."

"What does 'kowtowing' mean?"

"To behave in an obsequious manner."

"I could play this game all night, Mr. Snicket. What does 'obsequious' mean?"

"We'll have to play the game all night," I said. "I can't get the Bombinating Beast until morning. We'll return it to the Mallahans, and then we will find your father and defeat Hangfire."

I had hoped I sounded more confident than I felt, but when Ellington frowned at me, I knew I'd sounded just as unsure as I was that someone like Hangfire could be defeated. "How can two young people defeat him alone?" she asked.

"We're not alone," I said. "I have associates."

"The woman with the hair?"

"Other people."

"Are they nearby?"

I said nothing for a moment and listened to the piano playing downstairs. No other noises reached me. It was getting late. It was entirely possible that the person I was thinking of was deep underground. "Not as near as I'd like them to be," I said.

"You're a mystery, Mr. Snicket," Ellington said to me. "I've told you all about how I came to this town, but you haven't said a word about why you are here."

"I had an unusual education, like I said," I said. "My schooling is over, but now I'm an apprentice for S. Theodora Markson. Out of fifty-two possible chaperones, she was ranked dead last."

"You deserve better than that," Ellington said.

"I chose her on purpose," I said. "I thought that it would allow me more time to do what I really need to do."

"And what is that? Are you looking for your father, too?"

"My father is alive and well," I said, thinking with a shudder of the man in the Hemlock Tearoom and Stationery Store. "What I need to do is dig a tunnel to the basement of a museum."

"Whatever for?"

"There's something there," I said. "Something on display that needs to be in the right hands."

"But why do you have to be the one to do it?" Ellington asked me. "It sounds like a job for an adult. Why aren't your parents helping you?"

I thought of my parents, and then of the people who pretended to be my parents, and the eerie cloud that rose from the alley when Theodora poured out the laudanum that had been in my tea. I felt a complicated worry in my chest, like a tangle of wires or weeds, and when Ellington put her hand on my shoulder, I imagined that her long fingers would be good at untangling things. "My parents can't help me," I said. "They're helpless."

"Like my father," Ellington said quietly, and I allowed myself a few seconds to miss my parents very much. I thought of my father's face first, and then my mother's, and both of them were smiling. Just a few seconds, Snicket, I told myself, blinking very fast, because in a few seconds Ellington will ask you another question.

"But who are these other people?" she asked. "Some kind of club?"

"It's a secret," I said. "In fact, this whole story is a secret."

"If it's a secret, why are you telling me?"

"Because I like you, Ms. Feint," I admitted. "I thought you might find it interesting."

Ellington Feint gave me a slow, sympathetic nod, and we *clang*ed down the staircase together. Ellington pressed the *A* button to close up the attic and then rested her green purse on the counter while the machinery made her a coffee. I turned my eyes from Ellington Feint to the steam rising out of the top of the elaborate device. It was a nice thing to watch. The piano kept playing, and eventually I laid my head down on the counter. The last thing I saw before I fell asleep was Ellington's smile, and it was the first thing I saw when I woke up.

"Good morning, Mr. Snicket," she said. She had retrieved an orange from her purse and was peeling it with her fingernails, making a long, continuous strip of peel. I yawned and stood up. Ellington had draped her coat over my shoulders like a blanket, and I gave it back to her, although it felt warm when it was around me. Various parts of my body told me that in the future they would appreciate it if I slept lying down on a bed instead of sitting at the counter of Black Cat Coffee. I quietly reassured them that this was an unusual situation, and had the machinery make me some bread as a breakfast. Ellington passed me the orange and broke off a few bites of bread and munched on them.

"I was thinking while you were sleeping," she said.

"What were you thinking, Ms. Feint?"

"I was thinking that you were right. I can't trust Hangfire. I shouldn't give him the Bombinating Beast."

"So you'll help me return it to the Mallahans?" I said. "You promise?"

"If you promise to help me find my father," she said. "Shake on it."

We shook on it, hard. We finished our breakfast and left Black Cat Coffee, Ellington hoisting the zippered tube over her long coat and smiling at the piano on the way out. The sun was just beginning to rise, and Stain'd-by-the-Sea didn't feel eerie and empty, as it usually did. It felt peaceful. Normally at this time of day, I was sneaking a few minutes of reading before the morning began, and I wondered if Hangfire had those three library books that I'd wrapped in newspaper. We didn't talk as we walked the streets, just let the dim noises of early morning talk for us. A few birds, a few insects. Our own footsteps. Before long we were walking by the strange, unreadable statue and up the steps to the library. We went in the door as Dashiell Qwerty was shooing moths out of it.

"I was wondering who might come in at this hour," he said, looking first at Ellington and then at me. His face was blank as usual, but his eyes were curious.

"We just wanted to look something up," I told him.

"Make yourself at home," he said, but I was already leading Ellington toward the last place I had seen the statue. My heart beat faster as we rounded a corner of shelves, a loud pulse like that machinery at Black Cat Coffee. The Bombinating Beast had slipped through my fingers before. I scanned quickly for the location of *An Analysis of Brown, Black, and Beige* and pulled the book from the shelf. Maybe, Snicket, I said to myself. Maybe the statue is gone.

But there it was.

"Why did you hide it here?" Ellington asked in a whisper.

"A library is usually a safe place," I replied, "and this book looked so dull I thought no one would ever check it out."

"That's where you're wrong, Mr. Snicket,"

she replied. "This is the first book I would have checked out." The way she looked at the book made me remember what Qwerty had said. In every library there is a single book that can answer the question that burns like a fire in the mind. It was not a book on color, I noticed. It was not filed in that section. It was filed under music. I was wrong, though. I was wrong about which book answered Ellington's questions.

As she had in Handkerchief Heights, Ellington did little more than glance at the Bombinating Beast, and instead looked at her long, green purse, which she unzipped and held open for me.

"We can't go around town with the Bombinating Beast out in the open," she said. "We can hide it in here."

I looked at her, and she looked back. "OK," I said, "but I'm holding the bag."

I waited for her to say something like "Don't you trust me, Mr. Snicket?" but instead she reached into the bag and pulled out a small roll of papers, which she slipped into the pocket of her coat. Then she handed me the tube without a word, and I put the Bombinating Beast inside. I didn't say a word either, and neither of us said a word as we walked out of the library, down the stairs, and across the scraggly lawn. The statue was still lighter than it looked, but it was still heavier than anything I wanted to carry.

"If we take it back to the Mallahans," Ellington said, "won't Hangfire go after them?"

"Not if he doesn't know they have it," I said.

Ellington stared out across the lawn, although there was nothing much to look at. "I'm reminded of a book my father used to read me," she said. "A bunch of elves and things get into a huge war over a piece of jewelry that everybody wants but nobody can wear."

"I never liked that kind of book," I replied. "There's always a wizard who's very powerful but not very helpful."

"Oh, I disagree," Ellington said, and perhaps we would have had a good-natured argument then, which would have firmed up our friendship. We might have talked about books just a little while longer, and then perhaps my account would be very different. But we were interrupted by the arrival of a dented station wagon, with a red flashlight shining on top and the sound of an odd siren. As it pulled to a stop, I could see that the sound was not a proper siren but just someone imitating one—Stew Mitchum, leaning out of the back window behind his parents. Next to him was S. Theodora Markson, who was the first to get out of the car.

"Snicket!" she said. "I was worried about you!"

"Theodora told us you didn't come home last night," Harvey Mitchum said.

"Our darling boy would never do something like that," said his wife.

"We've had just about enough of this kind of behavior," said the male Mitchum. "We're not fools, Lemony Snicket, and we're not fooling."

"It's still too early to make assumptions," said his wife, "but it wouldn't be surprising if you were responsible for all the trouble around town lately."

"The burglary, for instance."

"And the vandalism."

"And the stealing things."

"I already said stealing things, Harvey."

"No, Mimi. You said burglary."

"It's the same thing."

"It's slightly different."

"Slightly different means almost the same."

"But not exactly."

"But almost. Almost is almost exactly."

"No, it isn't."

"Yes, it is."

"No, it isn't, and you have bad breath."

"That's not the point."

"What is the point?"

"I'll tell you the point."

"Why do you always insist that you know the point and I don't?"

"That's not the point."

"There you go again."

I hurried to the car with the point, holding up the zippered bag to stop their bickering. "I have the stolen item right here," I said. "There were some complications, but Ellington and I managed to get the item back."

Theodora looked at me in relief. "Is this true, Snicket? You really have the—"

"Yes," I said quickly. It was not wise, I thought, to say the name of the item aloud, even in front of officers of the law. If Hangfire knew where we were taking it, he would most certainly try to steal it once more. I was not certain who I could trust and who I could not. Stew Mitchum smirked at me from behind his parents' backs. I also did not think it was wise to unzip the bag to show Theodora the strange, dark statue that had caused all this trouble. I was wrong again. Or perhaps it did not matter.

"Well, we should return it to the Sallis family at once," Theodora said with a firm nod of her helmet.

"The Sallis family?" Harvey Mitchum said with a frown. "They left town some time ago. There's nobody in that mansion."

"Except maybe mice," his wife added.

"Mimi, mice aren't people."

"I know that, Harvey. Do you think I don't know that?"

"The rightful owners are the Mallahan family," I said to Theodora. "They've had it for generations. You can check for yourself in the library."

It was hard to say what displeased Theodora more, the fact that she was wrong or that she would have to go to the library to find out. "You may be right," she said, a phrase which here meant "I'm wrong, but I don't have the courage to say so."

"We can take you to the Mallahans," Mimi Mitchum offered. Her husband told Stew to move into the front seat, and Theodora, Ellington, and I piled into the back, with the bag scrunched between us. We didn't talk much on the way to the lighthouse, but the Officers Mitchum were more than happy to fill the silence with brags about their darling son. I would rather have read more about the silversmith with the burned hand, or the family making butter in the woods, or even the wizard who was of much less help than expected. Finally, the station wagon pulled up in front of the lighthouse, and Theodora opened the door and got out.

"You are no longer on probation," she told me, "so you can return it yourself."

She held out her gloved hand. For a moment I thought she was going to strike me, as she almost had the previous night, at the Lost Arms. But I was wrong again. Her hand hovered empty in front of me for a second, and then I looked Theodora in the eye and shook her hand as firmly as I could. Theodora winced slightly, and I turned around so that she could not see me smile.

"It's good to see this end well," Officer Mitchum said, waving his chubby hand in a happy salute.

"I was going to say that," his wife said to him sternly.

"Good luck, Mr. Snicket," Ellington said to me with a warm smile.

"Thank you, Ellington," I said. "I won't forget my promise."

"*I won't forget my promise,*" Stew mimicked, and began to chant a tiresome rhyme about Ellington and myself sitting in a tree. I walked up to the lighthouse door and knocked, and the door opened before Stew could spell out what we were doing in such an unlikely place.

"What's the news, Moxie?" I said when she answered the door.

"Lemony Snicket," she said with a smile, stepping aside to let me in. "What are you doing here? Who's that with you? When are you going to tell me what's going on? What's in that bag?"

"This is something that belongs to your family," I said, "that I'm returning to you."

She ushered me in and shut the door behind us. Her typewriter was parked about halfway up the stairs, and I knew that Moxie had been typing her notes in her usual perch.

"So?" Moxie said.

"This old gimcrack is part of a long story that I'm finally ready to tell you," I said. "I promised I would answer your questions when this was all through, so ask anything you want."

"Good," she said with a happy nod. Her hat

nodded with her as she continued up the stairs, thinking of her first question. "Why did you steal that statue, and why are you bringing it back?"

"I promised to deliver it to its rightful owner," I said, "and that's your family."

"But I told you that on the first day we met," Moxie said, leading me to the newsroom. "My family collected that stuff for years while the newspaper was in operation, but nobody ever cared about it except whoever wrote that telegram."

I took the sheet off the table and put the bag down among all the other paraphernalia of the legendary beast. "The same person who wrote that telegram," I said, "called my chaperone and pretended to be your father."

"And called me," Moxie said thoughtfully, "and pretended to be you."

"And called me and pretended to be Ellington Feint," I said, unzipping the tube.

"I guess he's good at imitating people's voices," Moxie said.

I stared out the window for a second, past the grassy cliff to the strange sight of the lawless Clusterous Forest. The forest was a lawless place, I remembered, but Hangfire would need to be someplace closer, where he could keep an eye on the people who were helping him. "Not just voices," I said. "I've also heard him imitate the cries of birds."

Moxie gasped and so did I, but we were gasping for different reasons, because we were looking at different things. Moxie was looking into the bag, which I had unzipped completely, and instead of staring at the strange, hollow eyes of the Bombinating Beast, she was looking at a bag of coffee stenciled with a black cat. But I was still looking out the window. The Officers Mitchum were standing around chatting with Theodora, and Stewie was looking into one of the trees with a wicked smile on his face and his slingshot in his hands. But some distance away, darting through the trees, was the running figure of a tall girl in a long coat. It was Ellington Feint, and she had something dark in her hands.

CHAPTER THIRTEEN

"So the butler did it?" asked Hector. It was his twelfth birthday. If there are any readers of this account, and I have no reason to believe there are, I hope you do not spend your twelfth birthday eating dusty peanuts in the lobby of the Lost Arms with Prosper Lost across the room, keeping watch. Most people deserve a party.

"Hangfire wasn't really a butler," I told my associate, "and he didn't really commit the crime. When his telegram to the Mallahans went unanswered, he hired Dame Sally Murphy to pretend to be Mrs. Murphy Sallis. He pretended to be her butler to keep an eye on her while she hired us to steal the Bombinating Beast."

Hector frowned thoughtfully. "And Hangfire convinced that girl to try to steal it, too?"

"Yes. He told Ellington Feint that she would never see her father again if she didn't help him. She broke into Handkerchief Heights and tried to think of a way to steal the statue, but she got lucky when I fell into her life holding it. When the police knocked on the door, she wrapped up the statue and a bag of coffee to fool me into thinking I was mailing the Bombinating Beast to Theodora at the Lost Arms. Ellington had the real statue and mailed it to herself at Black Cat Coffee, but I learned of the trickery and got there before she did. Then she switched it again, probably when I was sitting next to her in the Mitchums' station wagon, and ran off with it. And now we can't find her."

"Do you think she gave the statue to Hangfire?"

"I don't know," I said. "I hope not."

"It seems like an awful lot of work just to get a little statue," he said, "particularly one nobody else was interested in. What does he want it for, anyway?"

I looked around the lobby of the Lost Arms. Three days had passed, and they hadn't passed easily. I had spent my time asking these same questions myself while I read in the library or sat at the counter of Black Cat Coffee, listening to the player piano and hoping Ellington Feint might walk in the door. A mystery is solved with a story, and the story starts with a clue. I had thought the clue was the Bombinating Beast, but lately I had been thinking that the clue was something else. I thought perhaps it was the young girl looking for her father with nothing but a suitcase full of clothes and an old-fashioned record player with some tunes that wouldn't leave my head. I had no one to share any of these tunes or thoughts, at least until Hector dropped into town for the afternoon. "I don't know," I told him. "There's a mystery to the Bombinating Beast, and to Hangfire, that I haven't solved yet."

"And how much of this is going into your official report?" he asked me.

"Practically none of it," I replied. "As far as my chaperone is concerned, the case is closed. I simply wrote that our client hired us to discreetly find a stolen item and that both the item and the client have disappeared."

"That's not going to look good on your permanent record, Snicket."

"I don't care about my permanent record," I said. "I have a job to do."

Hector sighed and leaned back against the dirty sofa. "You're worrying everyone, Snicket. Monty's worried. Haruki's worried. This plan to choose the worst chaperone so you can secretly—"

"I don't think that's any of your business," I said stiffly.

"Did you know that two other chaperones were thinking of drugging you so you'd miss your appointment?"

"They tried," I told him. The Hemlock Tearoom and Stationery Shop seemed years ago.

"I bet you wish they'd succeeded. Then you'd be someone else's apprentice instead. Is Theodora as bad as they say?"

"She's upstairs taking a nap," I said, and Hector looked at his watch and shook his head. He was quiet for a moment, and then, with a quick and careful glance at Prosper Lost, took off his jacket and handed it to me.

"Sewn into the lining is the map of the city's waterworks," he said. "Don't lose it. It was very difficult to get hold of."

"Thank you, Hector. I appreciate it."

"I can't see it doing you any good way out

here," Hector said. "It took me all day to get here from the city. This is a strange place, Snicket. Those strange inkwells, that shimmering forest of seaweed, the masks you need to wear if that bell rings—something seems very wrong in Stain'd-by-the-Sea. I bet there's not a single decent Mexican restaurant."

"There's a good library," I said, "and a fine journalist, and several interesting people. That's more than most places have."

"Don't get interested in that Ellington person," Hector said. "She's a liar and a thief."

"She's just trying to help her father," I said, "and I promised to help her."

Hector sighed and stood up to leave. "You're in a real fix, Snicket. Good luck."

"Will you be able to make your way back?" I said. "I know of a good taxi service."

"Thank you, but I have my own transportation."

"Another ballooning project?" I asked him.

Hector nodded. "My chaperone has given me an assignment to take some aerial photographs of a distant part of the sea. Something suspicious has been spotted."

"So you're not going back to the city?"

"Not for months," Hector said. "Why?"

"No reason," I said, and shrugged my shoulders. I felt the packet inside my own jacket. I had spent the better part of the morning sewing it into the lining. Sewing is a prickly and boring business. Ellington Feint, with her long, careful fingers, would have done a better job of it. But it would be some time before I saw her again, and right now there was no use in giving my jacket to Hector, who would not return to the city in time.

"Good-bye, Snicket," Hector said. "Be careful. Please tell your replacement in the city that they'll have to take the long way round to the museum. If they tunnel into the wrong waterway, they'll both be drowned."

"There's no replacement," I said.

"So you're going to sneak out of town and join her?"

I shook my head. "I'm stuck here in Stain'd-by-the-Sea for the duration."

Hector's eyes widened. "You can't let her do this alone," he said, louder than he meant to say it. Prosper Lost blinked at us curiously and stepped out from behind his desk.

"What choice do I have?" I whispered to Hector.

"She's not just your associate, Snicket," he whispered back, putting on his hat. "She's your sister."

"I know that," I said sharply, but he scowled and shook his head and went out the door. I know she's my sister, I wanted to shout after him. Do you think I don't know that? Do you think I don't know I'm putting my own sister in danger?

"Happy birthday," I said instead, but Hector

256

didn't stop. It is possible that he was walking even faster. By now Prosper Lost was standing right beside me, and we both watched Hector disappear down the dark street.

"Fight with your friend?" Prosper Lost asked me, as if it were his business.

"It wasn't a fight," I said. "I just said the wrong thing."

Lost gave me one of his thin smiles. "Everybody does something wrong at one time or another."

It was true. Everybody does something wrong at one time or another. It was true, but I didn't like it. I nodded at him and turned away. The statue of the woman looked like she wanted to give me a shrug, if only she had arms. I shrugged back and thought about the other statue, the Bombinating Beast, and the villain who wanted to get hold of it. I thought of the fading town and the vanished sea. I thought of Ellington's green eyes and the question-mark eyebrows that hovered over them. It wasn't just one time or another. I had been wrong over and over and over again, wrong every time about every clue to the dark and inky mystery hanging over me and everybody else. It rang like a bell in my head—wrong, wrong, wrong. I was wrong, I thought, but maybe if I stayed in this town long enough, I could make everything right.